"I'm so sorry, Gab

"Don't. Just don't." He held up a hand as the familiar pain welled up inside him. "No one is sorrier than me. And sorry doesn't help." He glared at her. He'd had a lot of practice pushing people away, but regret flashed through him that he'd been a bastard to Rebecca.

Then she did the most unexpected thing.

Without saying anything, she moved closer and put her arms around him.

Gabe tensed, started to pull away, but she moved closer and tightened her hold. The warmth, soft and sweet, seemed to melt the ice inside him.

"I know nothing can make it better, Gabe, but a touch can be healing. A little hug can't hurt."

Maybe not, but it could be dangerous. She was so beautiful, her lips so close. The temptation was too much....

Dear Reader,

Four years ago, I moved to Las Vegas and noticed license plates from all over the United States—including Alaska and Hawaii. Apparently it's quite a melting pot. Sooner or later everyone passes through the most exciting city on the planet.

In *The Millionaire and the M.D.*, Gabriel Thorne relocates to Las Vegas to expand his successful company—and escape painful memories. Instead, the past catches up and leads him to Rebecca Hamilton, a gifted doctor with secrets of her own. They come together to help a troubled teen, and find that whether they like it or not life does go on. And love makes it worth living.

I hope you enjoy their story.

All the best,

Teresa Southwick

THE MILLIONAIRE
AND THE M.D.

TERESA SOUTHWICK

Silhouette

SPECIAL EDITION

Published by Silhouette Books

America's Publisher of Contemporary Romance

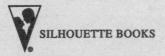

SILHOUETTE BOOKS

ISBN-13: 978-0-373-24894-0
ISBN-10: 0-373-24894-6

THE MILLIONAIRE AND THE M.D.

Visit Silhouette Books at www.eHarlequin.com

Printed in U.S.A.

Books by Teresa Southwick

TERESA SOUTHWICK

lives with her husband in Las Vegas, the city that reinvents itself every day. An avid fan of romance novels, she is delighted to be living out her dream of writing for Silhouette Books.

To Gail Chasan—it's a pleasure to work with you.

Chapter One

It wasn't sitting in a doctor's waiting room full of pregnant women that made Gabe Thorne want to put his fist through a wall.

He'd done it before—the waiting room. And the fist. But right now he was remembering the waiting. With the woman who had finally agreed to marry him. He'd gone to every prenatal appointment with Hannah, his excitement and anticipation expanding in direct proportion to the size of her belly as their child had grown within her. The moment he'd seen the plus sign on the stick, it was about being the best father he could be. It was about his child's brand-new life.

Except there was no life because Hannah had died and so had their baby. And a baby doctor's office was the last place on earth he wanted to be, especially with his unmarried, pregnant, teenage sister.

Amy was his parents' "oops" and had come along right

about the time he'd passed his driver's test. He glanced sideways at her, the sun-streaked brown hair pulled into a ponytail and away from her face. Big green eyes full of angry resentment looked back at him. An oversize T-shirt with the words Bite Me clung to her gently rounding belly. The sight brought back more memories of Hannah and a pain so deep he could feel himself being sucked back into the black void he'd just barely climbed out of. And once again, just like he had eighteen years ago when his mother died, he wished his sister hadn't come along.

Two days ago she'd shown up on his doorstep and threatened to run if he called their father. Part of him was okay with that, but he couldn't take the chance. There'd been too much loss already.

And just like that, more memories came flooding back—visions of the night before he was going to marry Hannah. After the rehearsal dinner he remembered following her little compact car, to make sure she got home okay. She'd insisted on driving herself because they were into the gray area of the groom not seeing the bride before the wedding. Hannah insisted it was bad luck.

As it turned out, their luck couldn't have been worse. The whole thing flashed through his mind again, in slow motion, like horrifying scenes in a movie. The car that ran a red light and broadsided Hannah. The god awful sounds of shattering glass and grinding metal. Within minutes, emergency personnel were there with equipment to get her out. Jaws of life? Not so much. Hannah was conscious only a few moments, just long enough to put his hand on her belly and beg him to save their child.

The baby was the most important thing.

So here he was with Amy. And he was angry because the sight of her brought back all the painful reminders of how very much he'd lost. But here she was and he didn't know what to do. Damned if he did; damned if he didn't.

Damned if it mattered because nothing did after losing his family.

"Amy Thorne?"

Gabe looked up and saw a young woman in blue scrubs standing in the doorway between the waiting room and back office. He and Amy got up and followed her down the hall and through the last door on the left.

"Hi, I'm Grace, Dr. Hamilton's nurse."

"Gabe Thorne," he said. "This is my sister, Amy."

"So you're going to be an uncle." She smiled. "Amy, if you'll just step up on the scale, we'll get your weight. Then I'll take your blood pressure—all the usual stuff. You're probably used to it by now. You look like you're about six months along."

Amy shrugged.

To Grace's credit, she didn't react to the attitude. After making a note in the chart, she said, "The doctor will be with you in a few minutes."

Gabe looked around the exam room, so similar to the ones he'd seen with Hannah. His chest tightened when he recalled those last times when the two of them and their baby had been together. He'd talked to her belly, telling the baby about baseball, football, how someday he wouldn't think girls were from another planet and that hamburgers would be a lot more appetizing when they didn't get processed by Mom first. In that little room decorated with poster-size anatomy charts and the blood pressure cuff mounted on the wall, he'd had everything he could possibly want. His fingers curled into his palms so tight his knuckles ached.

Then the door opened and a blonde wearing a white lab coat walked in, holding a chart. He did a double take because no way was this beautiful woman the doctor. Just like that, he felt like all the blood was sucked out of his head.

She looked at both of them. "Hi. I'm Rebecca Hamilton."

"Gabe Thorne. And this is my sister, Amy," he said, relaxing his fist as he extended his hand.

The doc took it, then shook hands with Amy. "Nice to meet you both."

If she had questions about the situation, it didn't show on her face—a practically perfect face with a sprinkling of freckles across her nose. And behind her wire-rim glasses were a pair of pretty brown eyes. He'd noticed a lot in a couple of seconds, including the fact that she seemed awfully young.

"I'm sure you hear this all the time, but are you old enough to be a doctor?"

She smiled and the unexpected brightness of it made him blink, then redirected the blood flow just returning to his brain.

"I promise I've taken all the classes, passed all the exams and done all the training," she said.

"You hardly look older than Amy."

"I am. Trust me."

Trust me? Not exactly words that inspired confidence these days. Maybe he should have done some research. Access to a recommendation would have been pretty easy, and now he wished he'd made the time to ask instead of taking an appointment with the first doctor who had an opening. But why should he be concerned when Amy didn't seem to give a damn?

He folded his arms over his chest. "I'm going out on a limb here and guess that you skipped high school and went directly to college."

"Not quite. Just a few grades with a lot of AP classes thrown in."

God help him he was going to hell for being a male chauvinist pig, and deserved to lose the hospital project that would expand the women's wing, but it was hard to believe a knockout like Rebecca Hamilton could be that smart.

She smiled. "One patient asked if I was playing Baby Doctor Barbie. You're quite the diplomat."

If she could read his mind, she wouldn't say that.

Rebecca sat on the rolling stool beside the exam table and carefully read the chart. "Amy, according to your paperwork you're six months pregnant."

"Yeah. I guess. I don't know exactly."

"She just arrived in Las Vegas," Gabe explained.

"Okay." The doc nodded. "We can request your records from your previous physician."

"She hasn't seen a doctor."

For an instant, disapproval flashed through the doc's eyes as her mouth tightened. "Is there a reason you haven't been to a doctor?"

"I'm fine. He made me come today." Amy lifted her chin and shot him a glare.

Rebecca met his gaze and nodded. "Good for you, Mr. Thorne—"

"Call me Gabe."

"All right, Gabe."

He wasn't looking for a pat on the back, or anything else for that matter. So why in hell would her approval and his first name on her lips make him feel... What? Something. It was weird. He didn't like weird any more than he liked feeling. If he had any choice, he wouldn't do either.

"It's hard to get medical care when you're on the streets, Doc. She ran away from home. In Texas," he added.

Amy gave him her best drop-dead-bastard look. "I'm eighteen. I can do what I want."

"The hell you can," he said.

"I can take care of myself."

"Yeah?" Her tone was surly and brought back that fist-through-the-wall-feeling. Her behavior was immature, irresponsible and he resented the hell out of her. He'd done everything right and lost his child. Amy didn't give a damn and had a baby in her belly. What was wrong with this picture? "If you take such good care of yourself, who was that hungry, scared little girl on my doorstep? Because she sure didn't look like a grown-up who doesn't need anyone."

"Time out." Rebecca stood and moved between them. "What about the baby's father?"

Amy's defiant expression pulled her mouth tight, and he knew she wouldn't tell the doc any more than she had him, which was exactly nothing. "She won't give me a name. But if I ever get my hands on him—"

"It's not your business," Amy snapped.

"No? You didn't get like this on your own. He needs to take responsibility. Why are you protecting him?"

"You don't know anything."

"You're right. I don't. And that's okay. But Dad—"

"Don't you dare. You promised." Amy's voice shook with the threat and her narrow-eyed gaze dared him to call her bluff. "I'm out of here if you call him."

He wanted to. He wanted to call his father and hand off the problem. He wanted her gone so he could go back to forgetting. But he knew if he made that call and she made good on her threat, there could be more he'd need to forget about, and he was already on overload.

"Calm down, Amy." Rebecca patted the teen's shoulder. "Do your parents know where you are?"

"My mother's dead," Amy said, glancing at him.

"Your father, then," she persisted. "He must be concerned about you."

"I called him. Gabe made me. But I did it from a pay phone."

"You don't want him to know you're with your brother?"

"No."

"Okay. We won't worry about that for now."

We won't? Gabe's gaze snapped to hers. He hadn't realized until that moment just how much he'd wanted her to order Amy to call her father. He'd been hoping for someone older, wiser, with more seasoning to tell his sister in no uncertain terms that she needed to go home. But Rebecca Hamilton had hung him out to dry.

"Wait a minute," he said. "*We* need to talk about this. I think—"

Rebecca gave him a warning look. "What we need right now is to determine Amy's general health," she said in a cool, professional tone. "We need to get some blood work. There's a test that will tell me the gestational age of the baby—"

"Ultrasound?"

"Yes."

He couldn't tell if she was surprised that he knew about it. For her the procedure was routine. Not for him. And he didn't intend to explain that he'd had firsthand experience. His pain was none of her business.

"Are you going to do that today?" Amy asked.

"We'll schedule it for another appointment. Right now I need to examine you." Rebecca's voice warmed and gentled by a lot, and she squeezed Amy's hand. "Don't worry. I'm going to take good care of you."

For a split second, his sister's sullen look slipped, revealing fear and uncertainty as she stared at the doc. "Thank you."

When Rebecca looked back at him, the warmth was gone, replaced by a cool, just-this-side-of-disapproving expression that made him uncomfortable. When was the last time that happened?

"I'll just have a seat in the waiting room," he said.

Gabe left, relieved to get out of the exam room, away from the reminders. But his relief only lasted until he took a seat in the outer office where several pregnant women waited. Some days he managed to forget what he'd lost but today wasn't one of those days and the future didn't look promising, either.

He cared about Amy. They weren't close, but she was his sister. Hannah had often told him that no one gets family right every time, he just had to persevere. But without her he didn't want to keep trying, and looking at his sister's growing belly would remind him every single day why.

Still something happened in that exam room—so quick if he'd blinked he'd have missed it. He was pretty sure he'd seen a chink in Amy's attitude and he'd bet his stock options in T&O Enterprises that the doc had something to do with it. He wasn't sure exactly how, but there might be a way he could use that to his advantage.

The name Amy Thorne caught Rebecca's attention as she looked at the stack of patient charts on her desk. She might not look old enough to practice medicine but she certainly felt old, she thought, remembering the scared, impossibly young girl with the defensive attitude. The teen had problems, one of which was a high-risk pregnancy.

From the corner of her eye, she caught a glimpse of someone in the doorway, and her heart jumped, then pounded as if it would burst out of her chest. It was normal for a woman alone to be nervous. Yet Rebecca's nerves always seemed to be running on high-test and hope was fading that the feeling would ever go away. The man who'd broken into her body the way a burglar breaks into a house had stolen her sense of safety, and she would always hate him for that.

"Are you okay, Rebecca?"

"Yeah, Grace." She let out a breath and forced herself to relax. "I thought you'd already left."

Green-eyed, redheaded Grace Martinson was her friend and combination nurse/office manager. When her practice grew sufficiently, Rebecca planned to hire more staff, but in the meantime it was Grace and her against the world.

"Still here, but if there's nothing else you need, I'm going home."

"Have a nice evening." Rebecca hesitated, then said, "Wait a second. What's your impression of Amy Thorne?"

"Mixed-up teenager." Grace frowned. "Now ask me about her brother."

Rebecca didn't want to go there, but participation in the conversation was easier than explaining *why* she didn't want to go there. "Okay. What do you think of him?"

"Above and beyond the call of duty comes to mind."

"Really?" It was reluctant duty at best in Rebecca's opinion.

"It's not every brother who would make sure his pregnant sister got medical care." Grace smiled. "And he's not hard on the eyes."

"You think so? I didn't notice," she lied.

"Oh, please. How could you not? He reminds me of someone." Grace snapped her fingers. "I know. The actor who was in that movie *How to Lose a Guy in Ten Days*."

Rebecca didn't need ten days to lose a guy. For her it was ten seconds, the time it took to tell her fiancé about the assault. Maybe not quite that fast, but everything had changed afterward until finally he dumped her. And that's how she learned that there was more than one way to violate a person's trust.

"I didn't see that movie. In fact, I can't remember the last time I saw any movie," Rebecca admitted.

"You need to get out more." Grace tsked sympathetically. "There's more to life than work."

This was an ongoing debate and a continuing waste of breath. Rebecca was perfectly happy, and it did no good to tell her friend that a personal life was highly overrated. She loved being a doctor and believed herself lucky that her career was deeply fulfilling. If she was a little lonely, well, it was better than giving trust another try only to confirm that the third time is *not* the charm.

"Weren't you going home?" Rebecca reminded her.

"Right. See you tomorrow." Grace waved, then was gone.

Rebecca picked up Amy's chart again and thought about the teenager. Definitely mixed up, but there was something about her. The flinch, the shame, the fear in her eyes when they'd talked about the baby's father. Rebecca had felt fear and shame once and wondered if she and her patient shared the same soul-shattering secret.

Or was she imagining victims where none existed? God, she was tired. She wished she could blame it on an all-nighter at the hospital, but she'd simply had a bad dream. The first in a long time. It was the noises in her new condo. That was normal when one moved to a different place. Right?

And when she could identify all the things that went bump in the night, she wouldn't wake up gasping for air because she was dreaming that same terrifying dream, reliving the nightmare of what happened to her. As soon as she felt comfortable and secure, the past would go back deep inside and stay buried where it belonged. And she would stop assigning a similar experience to a patient who'd probably just had unprotected sex with her boyfriend.

A shadow in the doorway startled her again. This time she ignored it. Without looking up she said, "I thought you went home, Grace—"

"Hi, Doc."

She looked up. Speaking of the devil. Standing there in the doorway was the noble brother in question.

"Gabe." Rebecca struggled to slow her pounding heart and get her breathing under control. "What are you doing here?" she demanded.

"Sorry. I didn't mean to startle you." He grinned and turned on the charm Grace had seen.

Rebecca felt a little shimmy in her stomach that was as annoying as it was surprising. She'd felt it earlier, too, in the exam room, a feminine reaction to his masculine appeal, but the doctor part had taken over and concentrated on her patient.

This time she was one-on-one with him. He *had* startled her, but that was all. She wasn't afraid. She couldn't be afraid of a man who'd brought his runaway teenage sister to a prenatal exam any more than she could help noticing how blue his eyes were and that his dark-blond hair could use a trim. Any woman with a pulse would find it impossible to ignore his broad shoulders, wide chest and flat abdomen in the white dress shirt tucked into a pair of well-cut slacks that showed off his muscular legs and great butt.

"I saw Grace in the parking lot," he said, his voice like warm chocolate and Southern Comfort. "She let me in."

"Why did you come back?"

"I want to know how my sister is."

"Amy and I discussed everything." Rebecca had done all the talking so "discuss" was stretching it. But she'd given the teen a lot of information. She took off her glasses and tossed them on the stack of charts. "Did you ask her how she is?"

"Yes. Now I'm asking you."

"If there was something she didn't understand, I'd be happy to explain it again. To her."

"I'd appreciate it if you'd explain it to me."

"She wouldn't tell you."

It wasn't a question. If he knew, he wouldn't be here, which would certainly make her life easier. But she was puzzled. Amy had gone to him for help and now was holding back. Why?

He leaned a shoulder against the doorjamb as he shrugged. "You know how teenagers are. A lot of it went over her head. She couldn't remember. So just give me the facts."

"I can't do that."

"Why?" he demanded. "I'm her brother. I've got a right to know."

"Not so much."

He blinked. "How's that?"

"Amy is not in a coma," Rebecca explained. "She's able to give consent and she's choosing to make her own decisions about her medical treatment."

"I'm not asking to make decisions."

"Right." She suspected he wanted to be in control, otherwise he wouldn't have come back for information. If Amy wasn't inclined to share it, why had she gone to him in the first place?

"Don't look now but your skepticism is showing, Doc. I just want to know what you told her."

"There are laws protecting a patient's right to privacy. If Amy wants you to know, she'll tell you."

"She won't say anything."

Then neither would Rebecca. She folded her hands on the mess of paperwork in front of her and stared at the baffled expression on Gabe's face. For a man who liked to be in control it wasn't a comfortable place to be. And why that tugged at her she couldn't say.

When the silence stretched out, determination replaced bafflement. "If possible, Amy's even quieter after seeing you earlier. I'd like to know whether or not I should be concerned."

"It's not that simple."

"It could be," he argued. "All you have to do is tell me she's fine. Or how about this. I'll say it and you just nod. One for yes, two for no."

"I can only say that this is a discussion you need to have with Amy."

"Who's going to know if you tell me anything? It's not like I'm going to rat you out. For that matter, I wouldn't even know who to tell."

"I'm sorry, Gabe." It occurred to her that Grace might have a point. He was annoyed, yes, but if he didn't give a damn he wouldn't be here after hours badgering her for information. Chalk one up for him. "Clearly you care about your sister, but my professional obligation is to my patient. I'm *Amy's* doctor."

"I'm Amy's brother. The way I see it that close personal relationship trumps your professional obligation."

What the hell did he know about her professional obligations? She sat up straighter. "What do you do for a living?"

"I'm a builder. T&O Enterprises is one of the fastest growing companies in the country."

"And aren't there rules you have to follow? Standards you have to maintain in order for the integrity of whatever you build to pass inspection? Obtain a certificate of occupancy?"

"Yes."

"And if you don't follow the rules, there are people you have to answer to. Isn't that right, Gabe?"

"You know it is, Rebecca. Do you mind if I call you Rebecca?" he asked, turning on the charm.

"Yes, I do mind." But she minded more that her heart had sped up again and it wasn't because he'd startled her. This *so* wasn't a good time to find out her high IQ was no match for his charm. "So you can understand that doctors have rules, too."

He moved out of the doorway and farther into the office,

stopping in front of her. She swallowed the familiar taste of fear. It was automatic; it was habit. She owned this problem. He'd done nothing threatening and she wasn't afraid of him.

"My sister left home without a word to anyone and when things got rough she showed up on my doorstep. In your opinion, is that sound judgment?"

Of course it wasn't. But Amy's judgment might have been impacted by trauma, and Rebecca had no intention of sharing those suspicions. "It doesn't matter what you or I think. In the eyes of the law, she's old enough to call the shots."

"She's eighteen. Just a kid herself."

"Even if you were her parent, I couldn't give you her medical information without her permission."

"That's nuts," he said emphatically.

She shrugged. "That's the way it is."

He stared her down for several moments, then ran his fingers through his hair, his frustration obvious. "Can you at least tell me she's fine? That's not actual information. It's more in the nature of how's the weather. How about those Dallas Cowboys. Or have a nice day. Just tell me she's okay."

"As I said before, it's not that simple." Rebecca couldn't tell him anything without divulging her medical information.

"What's wrong, Doc?"

"I never said there was anything wrong."

"Your face does. You're worried about something."

Was she that easy to read? Or was he just good at it? Or was he simply fishing for information? She hoped not—on all counts. Because she really didn't want him questioning whether or not she was nervous. Her jumpiness wasn't about the present, it was about the past. And that's where she wanted to leave it.

"I gave Amy all the facts she needs for now."

Facts like her blood pressure was high and a cause for

concern. The minuscule amount of information she'd been able to get out of the teen convinced her that when she'd eaten at all, her diet had consisted primarily of fast food, which meant too much salt and fat and not enough nutrition. Teen diets were notoriously bad, which increased the number of high-risk pregnancies. And a teen who'd had no prenatal care was at even higher risk. None of which she could discuss with Gabe. He seemed the type who would push the advantage if she gave an inch.

She stood. "I've said all I can. We have nothing more to talk about."

"Actually, we do."

"I can't imagine what." Rebecca stared up at him, way up. He was tall and muscular and very good-looking. A normal woman might flirt, but she wasn't normal.

"Doc, I need your help."

"With what?"

His blue eyes snapped with intensity, and his big body practically hummed with a nervous, almost desperate energy. "Help me convince Amy to go back to Texas."

She hadn't expected that. "I don't understand. If you planned to send her back, why did you bother bringing her to see me?"

"I knew she hadn't seen a doctor and that prenatal care is important."

All Rebecca could focus on was the fact that this guy's teenage sister was "in trouble" and troubled, so much so that she'd run away from home. He wanted to send her back and she couldn't believe that he had the nerve to ask for her help. Grace might be fooled into thinking Gabe was a noble human being, but Rebecca knew different. She'd learned to spot a jerk a mile away. Unfortunately, this jerk was a lot closer than that.

After what happened to her Rebecca had known first fear, then anger. She was clear on the difference. When she pointed to the door and saw that her hand was shaking, she knew without a doubt it was outrage.

"If you can't be part of the solution, then you should take yourself out of the equation. My office hours are over, Mr. Thorne. Please leave."

Chapter Two

"You have to understand, Doc—"

"Oh, I think I get it." She stared at him for several moments. "I'm pretty smart, Gabe." Pointing to her framed diplomas on the wall, she said, "I didn't buy those at the dollar store."

"This isn't about you."

"Or you either. It's about Amy. She's young and scared. And she needs her family."

"You'll get no argument from me. But it's her father she needs."

"Apparently she doesn't agree, if actions are anything to go by. She chose you."

"She's wrong. Like you said, she's young and scared. And not making good decisions. I'm asking you to give me a hand in convincing her to go home where she belongs."

If actions were anything to go by, he couldn't be bothered with his sister. Rebecca put her glasses back on and sat up straighter as she met his gaze. "If that's why you brought Amy to me, you've made a big mistake. I won't pressure her to do something she doesn't want to do simply because it would be more comfortable and convenient for you."

His eyes narrowed. "This wouldn't be about losing a patient and the revenue, would it? I mean, you're running a business—"

"How dare you." She stood up and glared at him. "I would never put business above the welfare of a patient. Especially the welfare of a teenage girl who's at risk—"

"Risk?" He tensed and was instantly alert. "What risk?"

"No, you don't." She'd let him sucker her temper into a twist and slipped up. It was a mistake she wouldn't make again. "I'll supervise Amy's pregnancy until her baby is born or she fires me, whichever comes first, regardless of her ability to pay. Is that clear?"

"Perfectly. And send me the bills."

"Fine. Then I think we understand each other. And we're finished."

"For now." The man had the audacity to grin but it didn't chase the anger from his eyes. "See you around, Doc."

"Not if I see you first," she mumbled.

And she wouldn't hold her breath about seeing him at all.

There was no question that he was good-looking, and she hated that she noticed, but Rebecca knew her judgment in men was seriously flawed, and Gabe was all the worst parts of mistake number two. If that was anything to go by, it was pretty unlikely that she'd see him around.

And yet she couldn't help wondering why he'd pushed so hard for Amy's medical information. Why would she bother to get her examined when he planned to pack her off to Texas? Probably to make sure she was healthy enough for the trip.

He'd shown his true colors, and any minute now she would

stop thinking about Gabe Thorne because it was a waste of time. Thanks to men just like him, she'd already lost too much that she could never get back. Smart women learned from their mistakes, and she was nothing if not smart.

Rebecca walked briskly along the sidewalk under the portico and toward Mercy Medical's automatic front door. There was a whooshing sound as it opened into the two-story rotunda with marble floor and information disk on the right, gift shop on the left. Every time she entered this hospital, the echo of hushed voices and hurrying footsteps surrounded her along with a feeling of reverence. The medical center endeavored to treat the whole patient with a combination of technology and compassion that healed mind, body and spirit.

When Rebecca looked around at the quiet beauty of the yellow rose painting on the wall and the words inscribed over the archway—Dignity, Collaboration, Justice, Stewardship, Excellence—her own soul sighed contentedly. Within these walls, she felt confident, fulfilled, at peace.

She stopped at the information desk and smiled at the older woman with glasses. "Hi, Sister Mary."

"Dr. Hamilton. How wonderful to see you. You're here for your workshop. Do you also have patients to see?"

The hospital board of directors had talked her into doing ongoing educational workshops to educate the public about the prevention and risks of teenage pregnancy. This was her third time and the first two had had dismal turnouts. Sister Mary was in charge of volunteers and felt guilty that Rebecca's time was wasted unless she also had another reason for being here.

Rebecca nodded. "Yes, I have a couple patients to look in on while I'm here."

"Good." The nun glanced down at a paper in front of her. "You're in the McDonald conference room again."

Rebecca nodded. "If anyone shows up, promise me they won't go down the street for a Happy Meal."

"I'm terribly sorry about that misunderstanding, dear. The volunteer was new. We'll make sure it doesn't happen again."

"Assuming anyone actually shows up."

"Someone already has. I made sure he knew the McDonald conference room was not a fast-food establishment."

"Thanks, Sister."

Rebecca's curiosity spiked as she walked away from the desk. He? Her goal was to reach teenage girls and prevent situations like Amy Thorne's. But it takes two to tango as the saying went and just because boys were anatomically incapable of carrying a baby didn't mean they shouldn't understand their responsibilities in preventing conception. Unfortunately, she'd found that an abundance of testosterone limited a boy's ability to think with his head, and they didn't normally seek out information voluntarily. So a *he* at her workshop was a major surprise.

She pulled open the heavy conference room door and walked past the chairs in the reception area. The McDonald conference room was divided into two smaller areas that could be combined into one large room if turnout warranted. Based on past results, she had no illusions it would be warranted for her.

When she rounded the corner into the tiny room and saw who her "he" was, she wanted to walk out again.

"Gabe," she said, hoping he'd chalk up her breathless tone to hurrying into the room. It was, in fact, on account of her heart beating too fast, something quickly becoming a habit when she saw him.

He was resting a hip against one of the long tables in front of a dry erase board. "Rebecca."

"How nice to see you again. It seems like only yesterday."

One corner of his mouth quirked up. "It was yesterday."

"What are you doing here?"

"I work here."

She wasn't born yesterday. "Really? Patient facilitator? As in facilitate them right back to Texas?"

"You have quite the sarcastic streak. Did they teach you that in medical school?" he asked.

"No. It's a gift." She readjusted her stethoscope, then folded her arms over her chest.

"Nice accessorizing."

"I like it." Unlike you, she thought uncharitably. "Seriously, why are you here?"

"To talk to you."

"How did you know I'd be here?" she asked.

"Like I said, I work here."

She was in and out of this hospital all hours of the day and night, and she had never seen him until two days ago in her office. "Doing what here exactly?"

"My company was retained to do the hospital expansion project."

With great difficulty Rebecca resisted the urge to smack herself in the forehead. She knew Mercy Medical was adding four patient floors to their existing facility in order to accommodate the explosive population growth in the Las Vegas Valley. She'd seen the evidence of construction—a portable trailer and signs around the hospital that said T&O Enterprises, but she hadn't connected the dots. For a smart woman she was *d-u-m-b*.

"I see," she said.

"Because of that, I'm in and out of the hospital. There are flyers everywhere publicizing community outreach programs—yours included. I figured it couldn't hurt to try again to get you on my side."

"And what if I didn't have time to do this with you again?"

He looked around the still-empty room, then met her gaze, a knowing glint in his own. "Yeah. I can see where that's a problem. What with the line out the door waiting to get in and hear Dr. Rebecca Hamilton's words of wisdom."

"I see someone else has a sarcastic streak."

"Imagine that. Common ground. It's a beginning," he said.

A beginning was the last thing she wanted. And when he graced her with a grin that made her heart palpitate, the wisdom of her instincts was confirmed. Her knees actually went weak and she felt giddy as a schoolgirl. She'd never felt giddy when she *was* a schoolgirl. She didn't want to talk to him again.

"My answer is still the same, Gabe. You're wasting your time."

"It's my time to waste and I don't think I am," he added. "Because, I have to tell you, it worried me when you let it slip that Amy is at risk."

She could understand that. "Amy can tell you what you want to know."

"I tried. She won't say anything."

"Do you have any idea why?"

"Not a clue." He met her gaze, and his own was full of flirtatious charm. "So you're not going to give me any information?"

"Nothing's changed. I can't. But I have a question for you."

"Okay. Shoot." He folded his arms over his chest and gave her his full attention.

All that attention made it hard to draw in a deep breath. Rebecca took a step back hoping a little distance would take the edge off her reaction to him. "Maybe the baby's father can get through to her. Did she ever mention him?"

"Not to me. But then we never talked much." He shook his head. "And since I moved here, well, let's just say nothing's changed. I haven't been in touch with the family as much as

I should have been, I guess." He shrugged, but the movement was more uncomfortable than cavalier. "I've been busy."

Doing what? she wondered, when he frowned the mother of all frowns, and the bleakest expression she'd ever seen settled in his blue eyes. Was it possible he really was worried? That brief vulnerability was the only reason she asked, "What's kept you too busy to keep in touch with home?"

"Opening a branch office of the company here in Las Vegas. It kept me too busy to think—"

"About what?" she asked.

"Nothing. Never mind." He met her gaze, but his own held lingering traces of sadness. "The building industry here in the valley is booming. A successful, multimillion-dollar company doesn't get that way by ignoring opportunities."

She stared at him. Cocky she understood, which was the effect he was going for. Arrogant she could deal with, although he hadn't quite gone there. Flirtation she was on guard against, because he was too good-looking for her not to be. But vulnerable? She didn't know what to do with that.

"I didn't mean to pry. And the past doesn't matter. What's important now is building a relationship with your sister. Get her to open up about what happened—"

"Hold it." He frowned. "She's having a baby. It's pretty obvious what happened."

Rebecca shook her head and only said, "Maybe."

His eyes narrowed. "You think there's something special she needs to open up about?"

"Not that she told me. And that's the truth," she added at his skeptical look. "Has she said anything, anything in passing, any hint, that she doesn't want her baby?"

He stood up. "Where did that come from? Did she tell you that?"

"No. But something's wrong. Do you have any idea what?"

He frowned for several moments, then said, "I'm not sure if this is on Amy's mind, but my mother died after giving birth to my sister."

That could be pertinent information. "Is she nervous about having a baby?"

"I don't know."

"You might try getting her to open up about that," she suggested.

"Maybe."

Suddenly all traces of charm disappeared and he looked angry, reminding Rebecca a lot of his sister. "How about you?"

"Me? What?"

"Losing your mother, especially unexpectedly from complications of childbirth, must have been very traumatic."

"It was a long time ago."

Rebecca had learned that what people *didn't* talk about was often as important as what they did. "The fact is your sister is going to have a baby. Did you ever hear her say she doesn't want children?"

"No."

He shifted his shoulders when he answered, as if he were uncomfortable with the question. Something was very off between these two and that begged the question—why would Amy turn to a brother who hadn't been there for her? It was a logical assumption that she believed he was the only one between her and the streets and she had nowhere else to go. In reality their issues were only Rebecca's problem if it affected the health of her patient and the infant she carried. But tell that to the part of her that was overly curious, in a very female way, about this man. She didn't like that she was interested.

For that reason she wished she could champion his cause

of convincing Amy to go home. But that crossed the line between professional and personal. "So I guess I've made my position clear?"

"You have." His mouth pulled tight. "And I'll do the same. If I can't convince my sister she'd be better off in Texas, then I *will* be involved. I'll be there for her."

Rebecca nodded. "Okay, then."

"So what *can* you tell me? What can I do?"

"It's important that she eats right. She really is eating for two. The baby will get what it needs from her and that will take a toll on her body unless she replenishes with proper nutrition. She needs to hydrate herself. No soda. Juice and water are best. Lots of sleep. And she's supposed to call the office to set up an appointment for an ultrasound."

"Okay. I'll see she does all that. What else?"

"Encourage her to share her feelings. This is a life-altering event. You haven't made a secret of the fact that you're not happy she's here. As much as possible, let her know she's not alone."

"Okay. Thanks, Doc."

When he put his hand out, Rebecca only hesitated a second before putting her fingers in his palm. It was warm and strong, and again she had the sensation of not being able to draw in enough air.

Since Amy had gone to her brother in her time of need, it was a good thing he had, however reluctantly, decided to support her. It was good for Amy, not so much for Rebecca. It meant she hadn't seen the last of him as she'd hoped.

But that was today. From experience Rebecca knew that tomorrow he could decide it was all too much trouble and that would be that. She'd learned the only one she could count on was herself and hoped her patient wasn't in for a similar painful lesson at the worst possible time.

* * *

Gabe turned his BMW right from Siena Heights onto Eastern Avenue and crawled through the congestion to Horizon Ridge Parkway. Wasn't it handy that Dr. Rebecca Hamilton had her office up the street from Mercy Medical Center? He had a portable trailer set up there for his office, which made it easier to supervise construction on the hospital expansion. But the short drive didn't give him a lot of time to plan what he'd say to the doc when he read her the riot act. What kind of game was she playing? He and Amy had their problems, but he wouldn't stand by and do nothing when his sister's medical needs were being ignored.

Just past the Radiology Center he turned left into the parking lot and pulled into an empty space. The desert landscaping outside the medical building was rock and shrubs—different from the lush bushes, grass and trees in Texas. But he knew from his last visit that the inside would bring back memories he'd done his damnedest to forget.

And as for Doc Goody Two-shoes, she talked a good game. Miss I'll-Treat-Her-No-Matter-What might look like an angel, but not so much. He had a bone to pick with her.

Inside, Grace was sitting in the reception area and smiled when she saw him. "Hi."

"I want to see Rebecca."

He didn't give a rat's ass whether or not the doc wanted him to call her that.

"The doctor is with a patient. If you'd like to take a seat—"

The last thing he wanted was to be here at all. Next to last was taking a seat.

"I want to see her *now*," he said.

Grace's eyes widened as she studied the look on his face. Apparently, she knew he meant business because she stood and said, "I'll let her know you're here."

Gabe paced in front of the reception window and noticed the waiting room was empty. It was after five and probably she was with her last patient of the day. Not that he cared if he inconvenienced her. She wasn't being especially accommodating.

Grace returned to the reception desk and said, "I'll show you into the doctor's office."

"I know where it is." He walked through the door that separated the waiting area from the back office and went down the hall, turning left into the room with the desk and diplomas where he'd seen Rebecca working.

Grace was right behind him. "If you'll have a seat, the doctor will be here in a few minutes."

"I'll stand," Gabe said.

The office phone rang and Grace looked torn. She picked up the extension and listened, then put the caller on hold. After giving him a don't-touch-anything look, she left.

He glanced around the small room, which was as cluttered as the last time. Charts, a computer and papers littered the top of her desk. On the wall in front of him was a seascape and another of a gondola gliding under a bridge on a canal, probably Venice. Apparently, she liked water. That was about as personal as she got because there were no photographs scattered around.

Before he could think about that, he heard voices in the hall, then saw Rebecca with a very pretty, very pregnant woman.

"Should I make an appointment, Doctor?"

"Yes. Although I don't think you're going to need it, Elena. I have a feeling the next time I see you it will be in Labor and Delivery at Mercy Medical."

The woman crossed her fingers. "From your mouth to God's ear."

Rebecca hugged her. "Very soon you'll be holding your baby."

"I can't wait."

Gabe's chest tightened painfully. The woman's pregnancy glow hurt his eyes, and the overwhelming feeling of emptiness and loss hurt his heart. And that was why he hated being here.

Rebecca glanced into the office, waved goodbye to her patient, then came inside. "Is Amy all right?"

"You tell me. Not only am I kept out of that particular loop, apparently further information from this office won't be forthcoming. At least not anytime in the near future."

She walked behind her desk but didn't sit in the chair. When she met his gaze, her brown eyes were shadowed and puzzled. "I have no idea what you're talking about."

"And I have no idea what's going on. Did you or did you not promise to take my sister as a patient?"

"You know I did."

"Then why was she turned away?"

The puzzled look intensified. "Again, I have no idea what you're talking about."

"When I asked Amy about her ultrasound appointment, she said she didn't have one because when she called there were no openings."

"That's not possible," Rebecca said, shaking her head.

"Define 'not possible.'"

"She's an existing patient. The next very important step of her treatment is an ultrasound. I want the test done stat—ASAP," she translated. "No way would she be denied an office visit."

"Well, she was." He folded his arms over his chest and stared at her.

She glared back. "She's your sister, but she's a mixed-up, hormonal teenager. And I'm not going to argue with you, Gabe. Grace answers the phone and makes most of the appointments. If she's unavailable, I do it myself. I'll clear this up right now."

The look she flashed him just before leaving the room was rife with irritation, and he had the absurd thought that she was beautiful when she was angry. He didn't like his next thought any better. He wanted to see what kind of curves she had going on under her shapeless white coat. That kind of thinking felt like cheating. Cheating felt like crap and was just another in a growing list of reasons why he didn't want to be here.

Rebecca returned, looking grim, a stark contrast to how she'd looked with her patient Elena. "Amy never called here, Gabe."

"What?"

"Like I said, Grace or I would have talked to her. If she'd called, we would have scheduled an appointment that was convenient for her or we'd have fit her in. Neither of us has spoken with her. I'm quite sure she never contacted the office."

He rubbed his neck. "Amy lied to me?"

Rebecca shrugged as she slid her hands into the pockets of her lab coat. "She's trying to avoid her pregnancy. The problem with avoiding your problems is that when you bury your head in the sand you leave your—"

"Backside exposed," he finished.

"Pretty much." The look she gave him was guarded. "The thing is, I don't know you and you don't know me. What we do know is that your sister is troubled. But sooner or later she's got to face what's happening to her. She ran away from home, but for her sake and the baby's, she's got to stop running."

"She ran to me and I don't know why."

"Me, neither."

Her look was wary and suspicious and made him feel more like crap than he had before. She definitely acted differently with him than she had with Amy, Grace or her patients. The weird thing is that he noticed at all. Since losing Hannah he'd been all work—no social life, extracurricular activities or interpersonal interaction. But through circumstances beyond his control he'd become responsible for his pregnant sister and was feeling a man/woman kind of vibe for her doctor.

He wasn't very happy about either situation. Ignoring this "thing" with Rebecca was a piece of cake, compared with ignoring the fact that his sister was going to have a baby. And Hannah's words echoed through his mind.

The baby is the most important thing.

"Okay." Gabe nodded. "I get the point."

"If you say so."

"Look, Doc, I'm sorry about storming in here. It won't happen again."

"Right."

Her hostility was showing, and part of him didn't like that. But he couldn't afford to care. One crisis at a time. Right now that crisis was getting Amy in here for the test.

"On my way out I'll stop and make an appointment for the ultrasound. You have my word that my sister will show up for it."

"Okay."

Her tone said she didn't believe him, and he wanted to say her cynicism was showing, but that would prolong a meeting that had definitely not been his finest hour. Actually, dignity was the least of his problems. The fact that he'd been tempted to prolong this meeting at all had taken him by surprise.

After stopping to schedule the appointment, he left the office and realized getting out of there fast wasn't as much about saving face as it was the fact that he wanted to pull sexy Dr. Hamilton into his arms and kiss the daylights out of her.

That was bad enough. Worse was that he had to bring Amy back to see the doc again. All of that begged the question: Which god had he pissed off, and what penance could he do to stop the harassment?

Chapter Three

Rebecca stood with Gabe in the hallway outside the exam room where his sister was going to have her ultrasound.

"What's going on? Grace said you needed to see me."

Poor Grace was getting worn-out being their go-between, Rebecca thought. If it was up to her she wouldn't see him at all, but she wasn't the pregnant teenager who was on the other side of that door waiting for a test she didn't understand and trying really hard not to let anyone see that she was scared spitless. Ultrasound technology wasn't invasive or painful, which made it an extremely useful diagnostic tool for gathering information.

Most expectant mothers were excited at the prospect of "meeting" their child for the first time. The majority of them brought along the expectant father to share in the joy. But Amy had no one, at least no one she felt she could count on. No one except her brother. And counting on him was iffy at best.

"Amy asked if you could be there while she has the test done."

"My sister?"

Rebecca smiled. "Do you know another pregnant Amy?"

"What I meant was—are we talking about the same sister who thinks I don't know anything?"

"That would be the one. I know tolerance is a challenge when she's been so difficult. But try to put yourself in her shoes."

One of his eyebrows rose. "Did you ditch those anatomy classes in med school?"

"Humor me. Just try to get in touch with your feminine side." Yeah, right, Rebecca thought. Could the man possibly look more masculine with his long sleeves rolled up, revealing wide wrists with a dusting of hair on his forearms. It was a sexy look and so far from feminine she felt stupid for even making the suggestion. Taking a different tack she said, "Try to understand that her body is changing and all of this is new to her. In spite of the fact that she's doing her best to pretend it's not happening, she's scared and would like someone there when she has the test."

"She's got you." The look on Gabe's face said he'd rather hike barefoot through a foot of snow on Mount Charleston than walk in that room.

Benefit of the doubt, Rebecca thought. Maybe he was one of those squeamish types who couldn't handle seeing a loved one in discomfort. During Amy's first appointment he'd known about the ultrasound, but the procedure was so routine that practically everyone knew the term, although not necessarily the specifics of how it was performed. A few of those specifics might help.

"Look, Gabe, it won't hurt her. It's a noninvasive procedure. I'm going to take a transducer—a wandlike instrument—and move it across her belly. It bounces harmless sound waves off the fetus and gives us an image that will tell me the approximate size and weight of the baby, and general information, possibly the sex—"

"She doesn't really want me in there."

He started to turn away, but Rebecca put her hand on his arm and he froze. The muscles beneath the warm skin were hard and unyielding, not unlike the man. Which made the unexpected flutter in her stomach all the more puzzling.

Ignoring the sensation, she said, "Not so fast."

The teen had been alternately passive, hostile and defensive. There'd been apprehension in her eyes and a tremor in her voice when she'd asked if Gabe could be there, and it was the first time she'd asked for anything. Rebecca had no idea what their history was or the nature of the problems between them, but he was the grown-up and wasn't getting off the hook.

He looked surprised as he glanced at the hand still on his arm, then met her gaze. "Not so fast?"

"I'm not letting you walk out on her."

One corner of his mouth curved up. "And just how do you plan to stop me?"

She removed her hand, then curled her fingers into her palm. "I haven't quite figured that part out yet."

She inspected the width of his shoulders and the idea of using physical force lost some appeal at the same time it produced even stronger stomach flutters. The sensation did not improve her odds of figuring it out and, in fact, made thinking even more of a challenge. What were they talking about? Oh, yes. Stop him from leaving.

She could share the fact that his sister was at increased risk of pregnancy-induced hypertension. Violating a patient's privacy would be a minor blip on the trouble scale if she couldn't get the teen to take care of herself. But she'd rather not break a rule.

She figured it was a positive sign that he was still there. "I'm hoping you'll just do it."

Gabe didn't say anything for several moments. Then his mouth thinned and a muscle jerked in his jaw before he simply nodded his head.

"Okay. Let's do this," she said, opening the door.

Amy was lying on the exam table with the head slightly elevated. She looked expectantly at Rebecca, then smiled when she saw her brother. Not a big smile, but it was the first Rebecca had seen. It was a start.

"Gabe, you sit there next to Amy."

He did as instructed and the teen started to reach out for him then dropped her hand when he ignored it and sat. Not a good start, Rebecca thought, when he rested his elbows on his knees and linked his fingers.

She walked around the exam table and sat on the stool beside the instrument. "This won't hurt. I promise." She gently lowered the sheet covering the teen's belly, then picked up a tube of gel. "I'm going to squirt some of this on. It's not cold. One of the really exciting advances in medicine is warm gel. Now, if someone could just come up with a way to keep a stethoscope above freezing."

This was a tough room and she was getting no cooperation in her attempts to ease the tension. One look at brother and sister told her the bridge over those troubled waters would have to be miles long. Probably it would be best just to get this over with. She picked up the transducer and pressed it against Amy's stomach, then moved it around, relieved that she saw nothing out of the ordinary.

"The baby is active. That pulsing is the heart—it's normal and strong. Everything looks very good." She glanced at her patient, who was staring straight up at the ceiling. Again, benefit of the doubt. Sometimes it was hard to decipher organs and limbs unless they were pointed out. She pointed at the image on the screen. "Here's a foot. And a little hand. See here?"

Amy said nothing and Gabe wasn't looking, either. He was staring at the floor and frowning as if it were a competitive sport. What was up with these two? She suspected she knew what Amy was going through, but Gabe's reaction puzzled her. Did he not like babies? Or doctors? Or his sister? Whatever it was, they were going to have to get over it because there was a life at stake. An innocent life.

"The baby has a very strong kick. Right now it's turned away, but if it moves just right, I might be able to tell you the sex." She looked at them to gauge a reaction to that suggestion, but neither responded, and she didn't understand the absolute indifference. But she couldn't make them care. All she could do was her job. The best outcome to this pregnancy was a healthy mother and baby and she'd do everything in her power to make that happen.

When she'd seen everything and gauged a due date, she moved the transducer around and typed in the command to print various views of the fetus. After wiping the gel off the teen's stomach, she said, "Okay. We're finished. I can—"

Amy pulled her shirt down, sat up and swung her legs to the side of the table before sliding off. "I'm going to the car."

Gabe stood. "Amy, wait. Dr. Hamilton is—"

The girl never looked back but simply opened the exam room door and left.

Gabe rubbed a hand over the back of his neck, then met Rebecca's gaze. "I apologize for my sister's rudeness."

"Don't worry about it."

"Hard not to."

"I'm concerned, but not about her manners."

His frown deepened. "What's wrong?"

"Everything looks okay with the baby. I was just hoping that this procedure would help her connect to what's going on, engage her emotionally with the changes in her body, help her bond with her baby. But she's still in denial."

"I guess I can understand."

"Then maybe you can tell me why she's indifferent to this pregnancy," Rebecca said.

"Why would I be able to do that?"

"Because you're acting the same way." She folded her arms over her chest. "Gabe, you wouldn't look at the baby, either. Is it possible that she's interpreting that as disapproval?"

"I'm not judging her."

"Does Amy know that?"

"You'd have to ask her. But like you said, what with all the changes happening to her, it's—" He blew out a long breath. "I don't have a clue why she's acting the way she is."

And he didn't volunteer an explanation about his own attitude, which unfortunately made Rebecca acutely curious, on a strictly personal level. The difference was he was in perfect health and not facing a life crisis like Amy. Maybe it was time to say out loud what she suspected.

"Is it possible, Gabe, that this pregnancy is a result of your sister being sexually assaulted?"

If she'd punched him in the stomach, he couldn't have looked more stunned. "No." He shook his head. "Absolutely not."

Two for two in the Thorne family denial department. Rebecca needed him to get it, but no way would she tell him her own experience was the source of her gut feeling. When she'd talked to Amy about the baby growing inside her, the defensive expression was replaced by a bruised look and she'd bet it was all about trust betrayed in the most intimate way. Rebecca knew how that felt. She just didn't know how it would feel to have a part of the assaulter growing inside her.

"Look, Gabe, I know you think I'm young and inexperienced, but I've handled a lot of pregnancies. They don't give you a license to practice medicine unless you have the training. I've seen a lot of reactions—from the unplanned pregnancy in a committed relationship to the infertile woman heartbroken when she learns that she will never feel a baby move inside her. In my experience, even the mother who didn't plan to get pregnant usually gets excited and is emotionally engaged when she sees her baby for the first time. Amy wouldn't even look. A child conceived through an act of violence would explain why."

He shook his head again. "That's just not possible."

"No?"

He loosened his tie with a quick and irritated jerk of his hand. "It's just... Amy... In your practice... Have you seen assault victims?"

Every time she looked in the mirror. Rebecca's chest tightened, but this wasn't about her.

She let out a long breath. "Yes. Unfortunately. Before, when I suggested you get in touch with your feminine side, I know you can't. Not really. And especially with something like this— Men don't understand what it's like to feel powerless. But it would explain a lot about Amy's apathy."

"If she'd been— If someone had...raped her...she would have—" Anger snapped in his eyes, making them a bottomless blue. "I'd like to say that she would have said something to me. But—"

"What?"

"But the truth is we've never been close."

"Maybe this is an opportunity to change that."

"The age difference," he went on. "And...other things."

Rebecca couldn't afford to care what those other things were, although she was curious. And, okay, she did care. But he wasn't eighteen and pregnant. Whatever he was dealing with would have to wait. The clock was ticking for Amy and she needed him.

"It's possible that this situation could bring the two of you closer."

For a split second amusement flashed through his eyes. "Has anyone ever told you that sometimes people just want to brood and be ticked off? They don't want to see the silver lining in any situation."

"I understand." She leaned a hip against the exam table.

He did the same and half sat, just inches from her. "I doubt it. You're Rebecca of Sunnybrook Farm."

Not so much, she wanted to say. But his words opened up a warm fuzzy place inside her—a place where she wanted to be a normal woman attracted to a very good-looking man. But... There was always a "but." And she'd learned there always would be. Her trust had been betrayed twice—first in body, then in spirit. There wouldn't be a third time.

She opened her mouth to say something, and Gabe silenced her with his index finer. In spite of her cold thoughts the touch made her warm again, but it was a heat that started in her center and radiated outward. She'd never experienced warm-and-fuzzy warm followed by wow-he-makes-me-hot warm. It was a one/two punch and she so didn't need it.

"I'm not Shirley Temple. I'm not an empty-headed optimist. I'm a doctor and my name happens to be Rebecca."

"So now it's okay for me to call you Rebecca?"

It had been okay since he barged into her office demanding that his sister get an appointment. The man might want his sister to go home, but he wasn't going to leave her out in the cold.

She lifted one shoulder. "You strike me as a man who does what he wants regardless of permission. Not a judgment, just an observation and none of my business. But Amy is. Like it or not your sister is having a baby. Make the best of a bad situation. It could be an opportunity for the two of you to get closer."

Rebecca reached for the black-and-white photos she'd printed of Amy's baby and picked out the best one. She held it out to him. Gabe took it automatically, but when he looked down, all the teasing vanished from his expression. In its place was a bleak look that startled her. He looked as if he'd seen a ghost, and she couldn't stop the question.

"Gabe? What is it?" She wanted to hug him. The reaction was instinctive and unnerving.

He set the pictures on the exam table as if they'd burned his fingers. Bleak blue eyes looked into hers, and his mouth pulled tight. Paleness crept into his cheeks despite the healthy tan. "I have to go. Amy—"

Then he walked out as abruptly as his sister. Part of her wanted to go after him and demand to know why he'd looked like that. But the part of her in charge of self-preservation held back. She had the horrible feeling that something deeply and tragically emotional had put that expression on his face and whatever it was had everything to do with why he wanted no part of his sister's pregnancy. She'd stopped herself from following him because if he wasn't the unfeeling bastard Rebecca believed, she could be in a lot of trouble.

She'd been shattered twice and put herself back together. She didn't want to find out whether or not she had the emotional fortitude to do it a third time.

In the hospital cafeteria, Rebecca bypassed the steam table with the day's specials and the refrigerated ready-made sandwiches in favor of the salad bar. Then she grabbed a cup and filled it with ice and diet soda. After picking up her tray, she carried it around the corner and kept walking when the cashier waved her on. Complimentary meals were a perk, however dubious, of doctors on staff at Mercy Medical.

Rebecca glanced around the sparsely filled room where people in civilian clothes mixed with employees dressed in different-colored shapeless scrubs similar to her own royal-blue ones. It was nearly seven-thirty and dinner was over. The cafeteria would close in about half an hour. She spotted a nurse she knew from the E.R. and walked over to her.

Kate Carpenter was a beautiful brunette with big hazel eyes and a gift for connecting with the patients who came into Mercy Medical for emergency care. She was alternately tender and tough, depending on what was needed, and situations in the E.R. could get pretty intense. It was important to have someone who moved fluidly between people looking for help and the doctors who made the hard calls. Rebecca knew some of them weren't easy to get along with.

"Hi, Kate. Mind if I join you?"

Kate shrugged. "Sure."

Rebecca sat down in the hunter green plastic chair across from her. "How's life in the E.R.?"

"Hectic. As usual." Kate pushed away her plate and what was left of her salad. "How's your patient doing?"

"Elena Castillo. Mother and baby are doing fine."

She'd gone into labor and come into the hospital through emergency. Kate was on duty and on the ball. She'd sent her straight up to Labor and Delivery. It didn't often happen, but sometimes an expectant mother got hung up with paperwork. Kate was good about making sure that didn't happen.

"Thanks for sending her straight upstairs," Rebecca added. "There wasn't much time to spare. That baby was in a big hurry. Her last office visit was three days ago, and I told her then that she wouldn't need another one. I was sure the next time I saw her would be here."

"And you were right," Kate said with a smile that showed off her dimple.

"I love being right," Rebecca agreed. "And now she has a beautiful baby girl."

Kate cut her apple in half then in quarters. "Good APGAR?"

APGAR, an acronym for activity, pulse, grimace, appearance and respiration, was the test designed to quickly evaluate a newborn's physical condition post delivery. It was done at specific intervals.

"The one-minute APGAR was eight. Not bad for a forty-year-old mother's first baby."

"Any reason she waited so long?" Kate asked.

"She didn't want to go the single mother route, and it took her a while to find the right guy." Her friend didn't comment, and Rebecca noticed the pensive expression. "Speaking of babies, how's your little guy?"

"J.T. is perfect." She smiled and the shadows in her eyes evaporated. "Getting too big too fast."

Rebecca didn't believe she would ever experience those maternal feelings, and that made her a little sad. She believed that a child should have two parents in a committed relationship and since Rebecca wouldn't commit again, she wasn't likely to become a mother. She knew her friend was a single mother, but not much more than that. "What does J.T. stand for?"

"Joseph Thomas. After his father."

"Joe—nice name," Rebecca said. "What does he do?"

"He's a Marine Corps helicopter pilot."

"A dangerous job these days," Rebecca commented.

The shadows regrouped and gathered in Kate's eyes again. "Yeah."

"Is he excited about being a father?" Rebecca asked.

Kate stirred her coffee without looking up and finally said, "He never responded to my letter telling him about the baby, so I'd have to say he wasn't happy."

"Is it possible he didn't get the letter? Maybe—"

"I don't mean to be rude, Rebecca. But it's not something I'm comfortable talking about."

"Of course. I'm sorry. I didn't mean to be nosy. I just— I wish I could help."

"I know and I appreciate it. That's just not a time in my life I want to dwell on. It's taken a while, but I'm okay." She shrugged, but the troubled look in her eyes belied the words. "I have a beautiful boy and will always be grateful to Joe Morgan—"

"Morgan? His father's last name?"

She nodded and a smile curved up the corners of her mouth. "It's who he is. With him around there's never a dull moment."

Rebecca picked that moment to glance over her shoulder and saw Gabe Thorne in the doorway looking around the room as if searching for someone. "Speaking of dull moments—"

"What?" Kate sat up straight to look over her shoulder. "Who's that?"

"Brother of one of my patients. President of T&O Enterprises."

"Isn't that the company doing the hospital expansion?" At her nod, Kate continued, "He doesn't look like a happy camper."

"No kidding."

Rebecca could count on one hand the times he didn't look like he wanted to implode something. Right now wasn't one of them. But the few times she'd seen him smile or grin were pretty unforgettable. Like three days ago when he'd been annoyed by her optimism. One minute his grin was a wicked challenge, the next it was replaced by sadness brimming in his eyes. The man definitely got to her and that was unacceptable. She hunched forward, hoping he wouldn't notice her.

"He's a nice-looking man," Kate observed.

"Nice-looking? If there was an APGAR for guys, he'd score off the scale," Rebecca said.

"Oh, really." Her friend's voice dripped innuendo like a leaky paper cup.

"What?" Rebecca stared at Kate. "I may be a brainer geek,

but I know a good-looking man when I see one. But that's all there is to it."

"If you say so."

"What does that mean?" Rebecca asked.

"Nothing. But your body language is speaking volumes."

"No way."

"Oh, yeah," Kate said, clearly enjoying this. "You could crawl under the table so he doesn't see you. Oops, too late. He just glanced this way and is now striding purposefully in this direction."

The next moment Gabe stood beside their table. "Your answering service said I could find you here. Rebecca, I need to talk to you."

"I was just leaving." Kate stood and picked up her tray.

He seemed to realize his behavior was abrupt. "I'm sorry. Didn't mean to interrupt. Miss—"

"Carpenter. Kate," she said.

"Miss Carpenter." He nodded. "Don't leave on my account. I just need a minute—"

"No problem. I have to pick up my little guy. Bye, Rebecca."

"See you later." She watched her friend's back for a few moments. Anything to put off the reaction she knew was coming, the reaction that always followed when she was this close to Gabe Thorne. She braced herself and met his gaze while the hum of attraction vibrated through her.

Taking a deep breath, she said, "So, why did you want to talk to me?"

"Have you seen or heard from Amy?"

"No. Is something wrong?"

"I hope not," he said grimly. "I'm afraid she's taken off again."

Chapter Four

It was a long shot that Rebecca had seen Amy, but besides his partner Jack O'Neill, the doc was the only other person in Las Vegas his sister knew. It was the only reason he was here when he wanted to be anywhere but looking into warm-brown eyes that reminded him of hot cocoa, a hot fire and hotter kisses. And wasn't it just more bad luck that those brown eyes belonged to a doctor. Doctors worked in hospitals. He hated hospitals. In fact, T&O would have passed on the Mercy Medical Center project if it hadn't included building two more campuses. Businesswise, it was an opportunity that would have been stupid to pass up.

"Are you sure Amy's gone?" Rebecca asked.

"She's not at the house and her things are gone. What would be your guess?"

Worry slid into those warm-brown eyes. "Did she leave a note?"

"No. Sorry to bother you, but I had to check." He started to walk out of the cafeteria.

"Gabe, wait." She was standing when he turned back. "What are you going to do?"

"Look for her," he said simply.

"Have you called the police?"

He shook his head. "I don't think she's been gone long enough for them to officially look into it. But I can't sit around and do nothing."

"Really? I should think you'd be relieved."

He'd have thought the same thing. And he would be, if he'd put her on a plane back to Dallas. But he wasn't a callous bastard who wanted her gone at the expense of her health.

"I don't want her on the streets." He turned away again and started toward the door.

"Gabe—"

He ignored her and kept walking even though he heard his name again. When the hospital exit was in sight, he felt a hand on his arm and stopped.

"Gabe, slow down. I can't keep up."

"Then don't."

"I'm going with you."

She was breathing a little faster from hurrying after him, and he thought she was about the sexiest thing he'd ever seen. Even in her shapeless royal-blue scrubs she looked like temptation-in-waiting. The want and need he kept in check around her stirred and stretched and snapped at the confinement. Since he was looking at the catalyst for this uninvited reaction, a catalyst that was making him crazy, the solution was easy.

"No," he said. "You're *not* going with me."

She tilted her head slightly, confused and curious and so cute his chest hurt. "Just like that?" she asked.

"Just like that," he answered.

"Look, you can't drive safely and look for her. You need another pair of eyes."

He would agree if the big, beautiful pair of eyes he stared into right now didn't make him want things he hadn't wanted in a long time.

"I'll be okay."

He walked out of the hospital and found his car in the circular portico out front. The BMW chirped when he pressed the button for the keyless entry, then he rounded the rear of the car, opened the driver's side door and got in. Just as he was putting the key in the ignition, the passenger door swung wide and Rebecca slid into the seat beside him.

"I'm going, too." She met his gaze with a defiant one that said she wouldn't take no for an answer.

Since the alternative was ugly, he said, "Okay. You can come."

It occurred to him that he was going to hell and had just taken the first step.

Gabe drove around for several hours through his own exclusive Spanish Trails neighborhood, surrounding areas and some of the rougher parts of town near Fremont Street. They checked the homeless shelters without any luck. Rebecca stared out the window and scanned alleys and sidewalks as they went by. She didn't say much, but his senses picked up every signal she gave off.

A single soft sigh slid up his spine and made his breath catch. The scent of her skin surrounded him, enveloped him, put a skip in his heart rate. A glance at her lovely, delicate profile fired his blood, sending a power surge to his brain that fried the rational circuits. And, not for the first time, he wished he'd locked his car doors when he'd had the chance.

He rubbed the back of his neck and felt her gaze on him.

"Gabe, let's take a break. You're tired and so am I." As they exited the 215 Beltway at Eastern, she pointed across the street. "There's a diner. We can get a cup of coffee and something to eat and recharge our batteries."

He knew she had a point when he was too tired to argue. "Okay."

He made the turn onto Eastern, then a left into the parking lot. After exiting the car, he rounded the trunk to open the passenger door as she was sliding out.

"Oh," she said, looking surprised.

"What?" he said.

"That's nice. Opening the door."

He shrugged. "My mother had very definite ideas about how a lady is treated."

"She trained you well."

"Yeah." When he saw her shiver against the chill January wind, he slipped his coat around her shoulders. "Let's go inside."

They sat facing each other in a booth, and he realized riding around with her beside him was a walk in the park compared to looking at her directly. As far as he could tell she wore little or no makeup, and the utilitarian scrubs were functional for her work, but not especially flattering to her figure. Again he should be relieved. Yet he found himself desperately curious about what she would look like in something exquisitely feminine—or nothing at all.

Thank God a waitress appeared and handed them menus. "My name is Julie and I'll be your server. Can I get you something to drink?"

"Coffee," Gabe said, and looked at Rebecca.

"Me, too."

"Coming right up. I'll give you a few minutes."

When she brought two steaming mugs, he ordered a ham sandwich. Rebecca took a pass on food since she'd eaten at the hospital.

When Julie walked away, they stared at each other across the table. Since he drank his coffee black, he couldn't even fill the silence with the activity of doctoring it up. Apparently, Rebecca took hers the same because she picked up the mug without adding cream or sugar and blew on it before taking a sip.

"So," she said, meeting his gaze. "Your mother is responsible for your impeccable manners?"

"Yeah." He'd expected her to ask about his sister, so the question surprised him. "She was a blend of tough and tender and I took the brunt of it."

"And you mean that in the best possible way," she said, her lips curving in a smile.

"Yeah. I do."

He hadn't had anything but dark thoughts about Lillian Thorne in a long time. Usually his memories were clouded by pain and loss and a baby sister who came home from the hospital instead of his mother. Remembering the tiny woman who would twist his ear to make a point, then make him bend down so she could hug him with everything she had produced a warm feeling inside him.

"It must have been hard when you lost her." Rebecca watched him carefully. "Bringing a new life into the world should be a happy time, and mostly it is."

"But not always," he said.

"No." She set her cup down. "So do you have any idea why Amy left?"

"You may have noticed she's not a great communicator. But ever since the ultrasound she's been even more remote."

Rebecca's eyes brimmed with sympathy and understanding. "Probably the reality of the situation is sinking in."

"I guess."

"But that wouldn't explain why she disappeared suddenly.

After coming to you in the first place, I mean. Does she know how you feel about wanting her to go home?"

Gabe felt the guilt twist inside him. "I'm not subtle."

One corner of her mouth curved up. "I noticed."

He remembered the last conversation with his sister, when he'd told her it would be best for her and the baby to go home, and that her father should know the situation. The last thing she'd said to him was, "Go to hell." "I might have pushed her some."

"I see."

He wished Rebecca would read him the riot act, tell him he was a selfish bastard with the sensitivity of a water buffalo. Her quiet disapproval was so much worse and he didn't know why. He hardly knew her except that she'd shown integrity, caring and a strength that was immensely admirable and appealing.

He stared into the black circle of his coffee and remembered her letting it slip that Amy's pregnancy was at risk. *The baby is the most important thing.*

The words raced through his mind. Hannah's words.

The woman he'd loved and lost. The woman who'd carried the child he'd loved and lost. The woman who hadn't survived to experience what she'd wanted most—to be a wife and mother.

"If anything happens to Amy…"

"We'll find her." Rebecca reached across the table and squeezed his hand.

Gabe looked up and instantly saw the determination in her expression. Anyone would have said the same to him, but the conviction in her voice made him believe. He hadn't wanted her to come with him, but he was grateful she was here. He wasn't alone and it was the first time since…

The guilt inside him knotted at the warmth of Rebecca's hand on his own. But it felt so damn good, instinctively he turned his hand palm up and linked his fingers with hers. He'd been alone for so long, going through the motions of living without letting himself feel. The grief was so big there'd been no room inside him for anything else. Somehow that was shrinking, the shadows were lifting, but the uncomfortable sensation convinced him that change was not a good thing.

He slid his hand away from the warmth of hers and hated himself for missing it.

"Gabe?"

"It's my fault she left."

"Has anyone ever told you that guilt is a waste of energy?"

He couldn't stop a smile. "Rebecca of Sunnybrook Farm. Were you a motivational speaker in between skipping grades in school and training to be a doctor?"

"No." She frowned, then looked down as she removed her pager from her waistband and studied the display.

"What?"

"It's the hospital E.R."

She pulled the cell phone from her scrubs pocket and hit the speed dial. "This is Dr. Hamilton."

As she listened, the expression on her face turned grim. "I'm on my way."

"What is it?" he asked.

"Amy. Las Vegas Metro Police brought her into the E.R."

As a rule, Rebecca frowned on shoplifting. In Amy's case, the right and wrong of it blurred because of the baby. She was caught in a convenience store taking food. The police brought her to Mercy Medical because she was pregnant and had fainted. Her blood pressure numbers were not good, and if they didn't improve she and the baby could be in a lot of trouble.

Rebecca had the teen admitted to the hospital and from all reports she was resting comfortably in a room on the second floor, in the Women's Wing. Rebecca was on her way to check her out before going home. She grabbed the chart at the nurse's station and checked Amy's latest vitals. Satisfied that all was stable for now, she walked down the hall to see her patient. As she got closer, she heard conversation coming from the room and recognized Gabe's deep voice. They were arguing.

This was a hospital, not the *Jerry Springer Show*. Her patient needed rest. Rebecca moved to the doorway and stepped in. With her hair pulled back in a ponytail and wearing a shapeless hospital gown, Amy Thorne looked impossibly young and still pale. At the same time she managed to look defensive and hostile.

In navy slacks, wrinkled white shirt and striped tie loose at the neck, Gabe was still rumpled from hours of searching for his sister. Apparently, his temper was just as rumpled as his clothes. Rebecca could understand it. His sister was doing an admirable job of hiding any hint of remorse.

"What's going on?" Rebecca asked.

"Gabe's freaked out. It was just chips and a soda," she told him.

Rebecca winced. If she was going to take food, something nutritious would have been preferable.

"It was stealing." Standing by the hospital bed, Gabe loomed over his sister and glared.

"I was hungry."

"There's a refrigerator full of food at my house, and no one would have arrested you for helping yourself," Gabe said. "And it's more nourishing than chips and soda."

Chalk one up for him, Rebecca thought. At least one of the Thornes was listening. If only that would solve all the problems. But there was a complex dynamic at work here and it was impacting her patient's health.

"Hi, Gabe," she said meeting his gaze as she walked in. "Amy, how are you feeling?"

The teen shrugged. "Okay. Can I get out of here?"

"So you can take off again?" Gabe asked.

"It's what you wanted."

"No." Gabe shook his head. "Amy, you scared the crap out of me."

"Oh, please."

"It's true. I care about you."

"I don't believe you. You've never cared about me."

"I'll admit we haven't been close. But you're my sister. I love you."

"That's a lie." Amy glared up at him. "Mama died because of me. That's what you think. You blame me for it. You've always hated me."

"That's not true."

"It is true. You can't stand the sight of me and couldn't wait to leave Texas. If I'd had anywhere else to go, no way would I have come to Las Vegas."

Gabe dragged his fingers through his hair as he blew out a long breath. "Look, I admit my feelings are complicated—"

"That's just a polite way of saying you hate my guts. Yeah, I stole food because I was hungry. But you're lying about how you really feel. Which one of us is more dishonest?"

Gabe stared at her for several moments, and the anger draining out of him was almost a tangible thing. He finally sat on the bed, weariness evident in the slump of his shoulders and lines in his face.

"You're not right. I don't hate you."

"Then why did you leave home?"

"You know why. To expand the business in Las Vegas."

Amy shook her head. "You didn't have to go. You could have sent someone else. But you wanted to get away from me and finally found an excuse."

"You're wrong, Amy. I didn't leave because of you."

"Then why?" she demanded.

"It was because of Hannah."

Hannah? Rebecca dragged her gaze from his sister just in time to see misery darken Gabe's eyes and pain tighten his mouth.

"Oh, Gabe—" Amy put her hand on his arm.

Apparently Rebecca wasn't the only one surprised by the revelation. Who was Hannah? He must have cared deeply about her. So why did he leave her? Or did she leave him? She couldn't imagine any woman leaving him. Gabe wasn't the kind of man who got dumped. The feelings pouring through her were symptoms of something that wasn't good, and she needed this complication like a bad case of the flu. She wanted to leave, but her patient's welfare could depend on understanding their complicated issues.

He covered his sister's hand with his own. "The memories were too much. I was finally going to marry her, Amy. Finally after wanting it for so long, we were so close to having it all. So close to—" His jaw clenched and a muscle jumped in his cheek.

"I loved her, too."

He looked up. "Yeah?"

"She was like a big sister."

"I don't hate you, but I resented you a lot," he said. "Losing Mom was hard."

Amy swallowed and her mouth trembled. "At least you had Mama for a while. I just had pictures. I never knew her at all."

Gabe stared at her, then nodded. "I guess I'll have to tell you about her."

"I'd like that," Amy said.

And Rebecca liked being right. Amy's pregnancy was turning out to be a bridge to a new understanding.

And, speaking of understanding, she wanted to know more about Hannah. God help her.

Gabe lifted Amy's hand—an awkward, almost rusty

movement—then cradled it between his own. "This is the honest truth. I came to Las Vegas because I didn't know how to live in a world without Hannah. It was too hard living in a place that had her fingerprints all over it. Texas had too many memories, and I couldn't stay there without the only woman I'd ever love."

Hannah died? They'd been talking in the past tense, but she assumed the relationship had fallen apart. It had, but for reasons that were so much worse than what she'd imagined.

Rebecca took it back. She didn't want to know this.

At the same time her heart went out to him while her respect and admiration soared. And wasn't that ironic?

She didn't want this attraction and now she knew it could only ever be one-sided. How stupid was she?

She was surprised that her impression of him had been so wrong. Gabe Thorne wasn't the kind of man who walked away. He was capable of a love so deep that he couldn't bear the reminders of the woman he would never see again.

Rebecca should have been relieved, but she wasn't.

Chapter Five

Gabe stayed with Amy until she went to sleep, then stepped outside for some air. It was late. And cold. But the cold in his heart trumped Mother Nature. He sat on the stone bench overlooking the reflection pool of Mercy Medical's serenity garden and waited for it to work, but serenity didn't come. He rested his elbows on his knees and clasped his hands between them. If anyone saw him, they'd think he was praying. They'd be wrong.

He never prayed. Not anymore.

His mother would be ashamed of him if she weren't gone, too. She'd been taken so unexpectedly, he'd never had a chance to pray. It was different with Hannah. He'd prayed for her with everything spiritual he'd had in him. On the corner of Matlock Avenue and Country Club Drive in Mansfield, Texas, he'd held her hand while the first responders worked obsessively to free her from the wreckage of her little car.

Because he couldn't do anything else, he'd prayed that she wouldn't leave him. But God ignored him.

Then he'd begged for the life of their baby girl so at least a part of Hannah would be with him. But God ignored that prayer, too. So now he didn't pray at all. It seemed safer, since he didn't think he could stand loving and losing anyone else.

Speaking of anyone else, he heard footsteps behind him and knew who was there before he glanced over his shoulder. Rebecca.

She looked like an angel, with the outside lights backlighting her, glinting off her hair and turning it into a halo. It had been a big mistake to let her ride along when he'd looked for Amy. There'd been a split second when he'd needed her, an instant when he'd been glad he wasn't alone anymore. He hadn't planned to talk about Hannah, and now he felt raw inside. The last person he wanted to see was Rebecca of Sunnybrook Farm.

"I'd like to be alone," he said.

"I figured that." She sat down beside him and looked at the pool.

He stared at her for several moments and didn't much like the feelings he was feeling when he did. "By definition, *alone* means no one else around. Solitary. By yourself."

"I know what *alone* means."

"Right. Because you're smart."

"Yeah. I am."

"If you were really smart, you'd take the hint and go away."

She glanced at him, then back at the reflection pool. "No."

"No?" He blinked. "No?"

"No."

"Why?" he asked.

"That's a very good question. Unfortunately, I don't have an answer. Except to say that I've never seen anyone who looked more in need of a hug than you do right now."

"A hug? That's your professional medical opinion?"

"It's good therapy. Never underestimate the power of a healing touch." She met his gaze. "Or a sympathetic ear. Don't knock it till you've tried it."

"My sister is your patient, Doctor. Not me."

"That's true. But I can't turn away when I see someone in pain. Talk to me, Gabe."

Sympathy swirled in her big brown eyes and seemed to pull him in. Really what did it matter? She'd already heard most of it anyway.

"Don't say I didn't warn you."

"I'd be happy to sign a waiver of responsibility."

Smart aleck, he thought.

Then he sighed and said, "I don't know when it happened, but I can't remember a time when I didn't love Hannah."

Beside him Rebecca moved, stretched her shoulders as if they'd suddenly tensed. He felt her gaze on him before she said, "Go on."

It didn't seem like there was more to say, but the words started pouring out. "The O'Neills—Hannah's family—lived next door. Her brother, Jack, was—is—my best friend. He's also my partner here in Las Vegas."

"Were the memories too much for him, too?"

"We never talked about it. When the hospital expansion came up, and along with it the opportunity to build two more Mercy Medical campuses, the deal was too good to pass up."

"And gave you a chance to escape the memories." There was an edge to her voice.

Until now. "Hannah was younger than Jack and me, but always tagged along. We watched out for her until we went away to college. After graduating, I went to work in the family business and waited for her to grow up so I could marry her."

"What happened?"

"It seemed our timing was off. She went away to college and fell in love with someone else. Married him."

"What did you do?"

"Moved on. Dated. But there was no one special. She was the one for me."

"But she was married."

"Until it fell apart. Then she came home."

"And you reconnected?"

"It was so much more than that. I was a man on a mission. By some miracle I got a second chance. I wasn't going to let her get away again." He remembered how long it had taken him to convince her they should get married. "Hannah was worried about making another mistake. She didn't want everyone to point and call her the diva of divorce. But I finally wore her down."

Thanks to her pregnancy. Hannah was seven months along when his campaign of charming dedication finally paid off. She suddenly decided she didn't want their baby born out of wedlock. But he couldn't say that. He'd ripped his guts out a while ago and it still hurt too much to talk about the baby.

"But she died before the wedding," Rebecca said quietly.

Like a surgeon's scalpel, the straightforward statement sliced clear to his soul. "The night before," he clarified and heard Rebecca's gasp.

"Oh, God, Gabe. How?"

"Car accident," he said simply, although there was nothing simple about it. "After the rehearsal dinner. I wanted to drive her home, but she refused. Something about the groom not seeing the bride before the wedding. She wanted to do everything right." He ran his fingers through his hair. "But everything went horribly wrong. I insisted on following her home. I had a front-row seat when that car ran a red light and broadsided her. I was there when they used the jaws of life to get her out and I went in the ambulance when they took her to the hospital. She died a short time later."

She put her hand on his arm. "I'm so sorry, Gabe—"

"Don't." He held up a hand as the familiar anger and pain welled up inside him. "Just don't. I'm sick of that. Her family's sorry. Mine is sorry. No one is sorrier than me. And the bitch of it is, sorry doesn't help."

He glared at her and felt like the bastard who drop-kicked a kitten. He'd had a lot of practice pushing people away and he was good at it, but regret flashed through him that he'd been a bastard to Rebecca. Then she did the most unexpected thing. Without saying anything, she moved closer and put her arms around him. He tensed, started to pull away, but she moved closer and tightened her hold. Words didn't help, but the warmth, soft and sweet, seemed to melt the ice inside him. She felt so damn good, and he missed a little of the warmth when she pulled back a bit and met his gaze.

"I know nothing can make it better, Gabe, but a touch can be healing. A little hug can't hurt."

Maybe not, but it could be dangerous. She was so beautiful, her lips so close, soft and perfect and there for the taking. Wanting her so badly made a mockery of what he'd just told her about Hannah. Finally the temptation was too much.

Gabe stared into her eyes as he slowly lowered his mouth to hers. It was a searingly sweet kiss that ignited a fire in his belly and sizzled through his blood as he slid his arms around her and pressed her to him. The feel of her against him drove out rational thought along with memories of the woman he'd loved. This was here, now, real and made him want as he hadn't wanted for a very long time.

He was sucked into a storm of sensation. The soft sound of her sigh. The feel of her slender body pressed to the hardness of his. The sweet taste of her skin as he nibbled the corner of her mouth, across the curve of her cheek and down to the underside of her jaw. She was like a feast after an eternity of famine and incited a hunger deep inside.

Gabe settled his hands on her arms, his intention to set her away from him. Instead he cupped her face in his hands, overwhelmed by the exquisite softness of her skin, the golden silk of her hair brushing the backs of his hands. When he touched his lips to hers again, the kiss turned tender and that was his undoing. Hot he could do. That he could understand. But deep and caring was beyond him.

He lifted his head and dropped his hands, severing the connection while dragging air into his lungs. Then he let out a long breath. "I didn't mean to do that. I'm sorry."

"Sorry doesn't help." There was a hint of hurt bruising her eyes as she stood and turned away.

Gabe watched her walk back into the hospital. He should have said or done something more, but what? He'd warned her and she insisted on staying. She'd initiated the hug that pushed him over the edge. The thing was—he did feel better, but it had less to do with the embrace than that lead-me-into-temptation kiss.

He hadn't meant to hurt her, but he was glad she'd walked away, because now he knew he could want someone again. It was a warning and he didn't plan to ignore it.

Chart in hand, Rebecca walked into Amy's hospital room. "How's the patient?" she asked.

"Ready to climb the walls."

"Okay. Spirit plus sass equals attitude. Situation normal. And a very good sign."

Amy huffed out a breath. "I'm glad *you're* happy. Me? I'm going bonkers in here. There's no one to talk to. Gabe promised to drop by and see me, but he hasn't. I called him a little while ago and left voice mail. It's not like he's far away. That portable he uses for his office is right outside in the parking lot."

Rebecca was all too aware of that. And him.

The potential for a Gabe sighting was never far from her mind because that little portable he used for an office was practically close enough to hit with a rock.

"He's probably very busy, Amy." Rebecca moved farther into the room and stood at the foot of the bed. "The hospital construction is a lot for him to deal with."

"And now me." Hostility and resentment snapped in her voice. And hurt simmered just below the surface.

"He cares, kiddo. You should have seen how worried he was when he couldn't find you."

"Really?"

Rebecca nodded. "He tracked me down here at the hospital to see if I'd heard from you. Then we spent the next few hours driving around looking."

"After last night when we talked, I—" She shrugged. "I guess I was looking forward to him visiting."

The words tugged at Rebecca's heart. Amy was putting a lot of energy into pretending she didn't care about anything or anyone at the same time she desperately wanted support and love. As a doctor, Rebecca could support her and give her the best possible medical care. But a brother's love could only come from Gabe.

"That's one of the things I'm here to tell you. Visitors won't be necessary because I'm discharging you."

"Awesome."

"However—" Rebecca stopped when the teen groaned. "I want your word you're going to take care of yourself. No more running away. No chips and soda for meals. Fruits, vegetables, protein. I want your solemn vow."

A gleam stole into Amy's eyes. "I'll promise. If you'll do something for me."

"What?"

"Make Gabe come and get me out of here now."

"I'm sure he'll be here as soon as he can, to take you home. Relax. It's not hospital policy to put you on the curb with your suitcase until your ride comes."

"I know. It's just— I'm anxious to go. No offense."

"None taken."

Amy looked intense. "The thing is, he'll listen if you see him face-to-face."

Face-to-face was the last thing Rebecca wanted. It scared the living daylights out of her after last night. They'd been *face-to-face*, or more accurately, mouth to mouth. And there was no resuscitating going on. Except that wasn't completely true when talking hormones. He had definitely breathed new life into hers.

She shouldn't have let him kiss her. She'd known he was going to and meant to stop him. But she'd been mesmerized into immobility by the intensity in his eyes. She could deny the truth until hell wouldn't have it, but the fact was she'd wanted him to kiss her. In spite of just learning that he would never love again.

She'd never been good at the social stuff. In fact for a while she'd blamed herself for the assault. If she'd had street smarts instead of book smarts, maybe it wouldn't have happened. Eventually she'd understood that it's assault when a guy doesn't take no for an answer. And she definitely hadn't said no to Gabe. He would have respected it; he was a good man. This would be so much easier if he wasn't. How she wished she could trade IQ points for social skills.

"Hey. Earth to doc—"

"What?" She blinked her patient into focus. "Sorry. I've got something on my mind."

"Does it have anything to do with the fact that I can't get out of here until my brother comes to get me?"

"No." Rebecca grinned. "It has to do with you cleaning up your act—in a nutritional way. But I will hunt your brother down and give him the four-one-one."

As it turned out she didn't have far to go. After leaving Amy's room, Rebecca replaced the chart at the nurse's station, then glanced to her left down the corridor and spotted a familiar pair of broad shoulders. He was staring through the glass doors that separated patient rooms from the newborn nursery.

She wondered how she'd recognized him so quickly. Especially from the back. There was, of course, the exceptional butt. A part of the anatomy she hadn't truly appreciated when she'd taken the course. Not until meeting Gabe had her opinion in that regard changed. And recognizing the folly of seeing him more than necessary, she'd resolved to stay out of his way. Except, now she was on an errand for her patient.

She walked down the hall and stopped beside him. Lost in his own thoughts, he didn't say anything, but she'd have given a lot to know what he was thinking, why the signs of sorrow were deeper on his face. Was this about his sister's baby? They'd never talked again about how the baby was conceived, who the father was, and that could be on his mind. Whatever was bothering him, she couldn't stand to see him look that way.

"Gabe?"

He glanced at her and there was no warm, gooey expression that usually followed when someone looked at the babies. Gabe's eyes were hard and there was a coldness that made her shiver.

"What's wrong?"

"I hate hospitals."

And that told her everything. He was thinking about Hannah. Losing her. And the patient rooms, long corridors and antiseptic environment reminded him of what he'd lost. She could tell him how many people were helped every day, how many were better off for medical intervention, but he wouldn't want to hear it. She thought about pointing out that the babies on the other side of these doors were thriving and healthy and would be going home to start their lives. The expression in his eyes dared her to say something optimistic so he could mock her.

Instead she said, "Then you've got a problem."

"How's that?"

"Since you're building on to this one, you work here."

"It's different when it's just a shell. Without people."

"People benefit from the good work that happens within the walls you put up."

"And a lot of bad happens," he said.

She knew he couldn't let go of Hannah. "We can't save everyone. But how many more people would be lost without the benefit of this facility and others like it?"

He blew out a long breath and met her gaze. "That doesn't mean I'll ever be comfortable here."

"Most people aren't. I happen to find the environment invigorating as well as serene."

"Then you're a sick woman." A hint of humor replaced the hardness in his eyes, and a smile took the sting from the words.

"Thank you," she said, then remembered her errand. "Considering your aversion to hospitals, isn't it handy that I found you here."

"Were you looking for me?" he asked.

She nodded. "Your sister asked me to."

"How's she doing?"

"I'm discharging her."

"Okay. Good," he said, but the tone in his voice said the news was anything but.

"What's going on? I thought you two connected and bonded earlier."

"We did. It's just—" He glanced at the newborns just beyond them.

"She's having a baby," Rebecca guessed. "And that's a lot of responsibility."

"Something like that," he admitted.

"If you feel that way, imagine how scared she is."

"I thought we already established that I don't have a clue about what she's feeling."

"You don't really have to. All she wants is for you to be there for her. Medical training and medicine can only do so much. Doctors are still puzzled by the miracles they see due to the human spirit and other things that science can't explain."

"What are you saying?"

"I need your help to help your sister. I can only do so much. The rest is up to her and for that she needs you."

He rubbed a hand over the back of his neck. "I don't know if—"

"Stop right there. I'm sure it was hard losing Hannah." The frown darkening his expression didn't deter her. "The bad stuff sucks. When you use every trick you've learned, every skill you have, work as hard as you can and throw in a prayer because you've got nothing left, and you still lose someone, that always sucks."

"Then why do you do it?"

He would probably mock her, but he'd asked and she'd tell the truth.

"I do it because of the ones who get better. Because of my skill, luck, prayers, the strength of my patients and their families, they get to have a life. A first day of kindergarten. High school. The prom. A healthy baby of their own one day. And miracles do happen, just not always when we want them to. But I take them wherever I can find them. When I get one, I reach out and grab it and thank science and logic and the Powers That Be that I touched someone in a positive way." She planted her hands on her hips and stared defiantly up at him. "That's why."

"Good answer."

"There's more. Amy needs you now. She said if she'd had anywhere else to go, she wouldn't have come to Las Vegas. But I think it's more than that. Instinctively she knew you were the one she wanted to support her through this time in her life. I don't mean to sound callous, but it's time to put loss in the past and focus on life."

To take the sting out of her words, Rebecca put her hand on his arm. It was a mistake. She felt the heat of his skin through the material of his white dress shirt. And he wasn't frowning anymore. The shadows disappeared, burned away by the heat in his eyes. In fact, he was looking at her the same way he had before he'd kissed her. Her stomach dropped as if she were riding the Insanity ride at the top of the Stratosphere and her heart started pounding. Every visceral response to him was multiplied by ten when he put his big, warm hand over hers.

"Did you ever think about becoming a lawyer?" he asked.

"N-no. Why?"

"Because you're very persuasive. I don't believe that I have anything to offer my sister, but you've put a reasonable doubt in my mind."

"Good, I—"

"The fact is, if you stand there any longer looking at me with those amazing eyes and wearing your passion and dedication on your sleeve, I would promise you anything."

Rebecca met his gaze and barely registered the fact that she was glad his eyes weren't sad anymore. Then she struggled for nonchalance. Indifference equaled survival.

To become a doctor she'd taken an oath to do no harm, and constantly balanced watching and waiting with intervention in a patient's care. But doing no harm to herself was far more complicated. Especially when Gabe Thorne grinned the grin that made her knees go weak. The grin that made her forget he was sorry he'd kissed her. She couldn't be sorry for it and knew that attitude would get her hurt again.

Unless she could make these feelings go away, this man could do her a whole lot of harm.

Chapter Six

Gabe stared at the budget report on his desk and made another attempt to absorb the contents. But the harder he looked, the more the figures turned into a pair of big brown eyes that sparkled with tenderness and humor. Or a smile that made him warm all over. Or a frown of disappointment that made him want to take back something he'd said.

He shook his head and considered the report again because Jack O'Neill sat in a chair across from him. Since branching out in Las Vegas, they'd set up their office in a triple-wide portable on land adjacent to Mercy Medical. They each had an administrative assistant and funneled a lot of paperwork through the corporate office in Dallas.

Once a week he had a project status meeting with his partner to go over current and future projects of Thorne & O'Neill, but concentrating had never been this hard before. In fact, Gabe made it a priority to focus completely on business because he didn't want to think about anything else. Suddenly everything else was crowding in anyway, and he didn't like it.

Gabe looked at his friend. "Give me the highlights."

"You know the price of steel has gone up." With a puzzled frown on his face, Jack stared back. "It's all there."

"Okay," he answered absently.

Jack was more than a friend to him and they'd been pretty much inseparable from the time the Thornes had bought a house in the exclusive gated community and moved next door to the O'Neills when Gabe was ten. Hannah had adored her older brother Jack. When she was little, she'd been the pain-in-the-ass tagalong. She grew up and teased Jack about being the tall, dark, handsome Hollywood-leading-man type who left a trail of broken hearts wherever he went. Women wanted to marry him and men wanted to be his best friend. Gabe couldn't remember a time when Jack wasn't his friend.

Football. Discovering girls. Their first drink, first drunk, first hangover. College. Becoming business partners. Jack had always been there. Losing Hannah was no exception. If not for Jack... Gabe didn't even want to go there.

"The price of cement has gone up, too." Jack shifted the papers in front of him.

"I see."

Speaking of seeing, he hadn't seen Rebecca since Amy had been discharged from the hospital. That was two weeks ago, and things had been pretty quiet. At least with him and his sister. With him and his thoughts, not so much. Kissing the doctor was never far from his mind. What the hell had he been thinking?

Jack cleared his throat. "Fortunately, we factored inflation costs for materials into our bid for the hospital expansion, so we're still okay."

"That's too bad."

Gabe barely registered Jack's words because he was too busy remembering the feel of Rebecca's hand on his arm when she said what got her through was helping the patients she could. She'd argued passionately that he had a lot of support to offer his sister. Her touch had pulled him back from the dark place he'd gone, after looking at the babies in the newborn nursery. Her passion was a tangible force. When he wondered about channeling that force in his direction, a shaft of heat went straight through him.

Jack loudly cleared his throat. "I'm going to sell you my half of the business and become a monk."

"Good." The word *monk* finally penetrated, and Gabe looked up sharply. "What?"

"Now that I have your attention…"

"Sorry. I'm distracted this morning."

"Just this morning?" Jack shook his head.

"Okay, maybe a little longer."

"A little longer? Get real. Buddy, your head hasn't been in the game for a while now. I don't need to remind you that this is an important project for the company."

"I'm aware of that," Gabe snapped.

"We've been working pretty hard," Jack said slowly, studying him. "Maybe we should take off for a long weekend. A ski trip to Utah would clear your head. It's not that far and—"

"I can't."

Gabe stood and walked to the window, his footsteps heavy and hollow on the floor of the manufactured portable. The walls were paneled and carpet covered the floor, but it was still a temporary setup.

"Okay," Jack said. "That's it. I've given you space, but no more mister nice guy. What the hell is going on with you? And don't tell me nothing."

Gabe stared out at the nearby foothills, green from a recent rain. "I didn't think it showed."

There was a long-suffering sigh behind him. "This is me, buddy."

He turned and shrugged. "Yeah."

"Give it up."

About Rebecca he didn't know where to start. So he went with the most obvious of two revelations.

"Amy's in Vegas."

"Okay." Jack's gaze narrowed. "Is this a good surprise?"

"The part where she showed up without warning? Or the part where she's pregnant?"

Jack straightened in his chair. The normally unflappable man was clearly shocked. "Little Amy is having a baby? Wow. I don't know what to say."

"Join the club."

"How's your dad taking all this?" Jack asked.

"He doesn't know."

"What?"

"Oh, he knows she's all right, but she won't tell him where she is."

"Does he know about the baby?"

Gabe shook his head. "And she won't let me tell him. Says she'll take off again if I do. And the doctor says she's at risk—"

"At risk? How? She's a teenager. In the best shape of her life."

"Apparently not. I've done a little research, and teens tend not to take care of themselves."

"Why did you have to do research? She's under a doctor's care."

"There's a privacy thing between doctor and patient, and medical information can't be revealed without permission."

"Amy won't give it?"

"Right in one." Gabe leaned a hip against his desk. "And the doc won't break the rules."

"What *did* the doc tell you?"

"She said—"

"She?"

This would be a good place to insert not-so-obvious revelation number two. Rebecca. But what did he say? That he was feeling lust for another woman besides Hannah? He couldn't reconcile that for himself let alone say it out loud to her brother.

"Dr. Rebecca Hamilton. She said to make sure Amy eats right. Gets enough rest." He dragged his fingers through his hair. "But—"

"You want her back in Texas."

"I want what's best for her." For the record, he still didn't believe that was him.

"Do you know why she won't go?"

"No idea why she insists on staying here with me. When I put some pressure on her to go home, she took off again. And landed in the hospital."

"Is she okay?"

"She's stable. For now," Gabe added. "In fact, she has an appointment with Rebecca later this afternoon."

To make sure she was okay physically, Gabe thought. Emotionally was something else. Amy wasn't the carefree sister he remembered. He hadn't known her well, but she was definitely different, and Rebecca had a theory about that. He trusted her with Amy's medical care, but still couldn't figure out why she'd jumped to the conclusion that his sister was a victim of sexual assault. The thought of it sent hot-and-cold-running anger through him. Gabe decided not to share the speculation.

"Is there some reason you felt you needed to carry this around by yourself?" Jack stood and met his gaze.

"It's not about that. I just—" He didn't want to talk about

why he didn't want to talk about it. "Let's just move on. About that report—"

"Not so fast. Why didn't you tell me about this?"

"Jack, let it go."

His friend shook his head. "No way. Say it, Gabe. Why?"

Gabe stared for a long moment then said, "A pregnant sister. I guess—" He blew out a long breath. "Because I didn't want to remind you about Hannah."

"Okay." Jack's mouth thinned for a moment, then he nodded. "Here's the thing. She was my sister. I loved her and I'll miss her for the rest of my life. But you lost the woman you love and your child."

The woman who would never have a baby. The child who would never have a first day in kindergarten. Rebecca was right. It sucked. And the fact she understood that better than anyone should have made him feel better, but it didn't.

"What's this situation doing to *your* memories?" Jack asked.

Gabe shook his head, remembering the painful feelings during that first appointment with his sister. Since then, somehow, his attention had shifted. To Rebecca. "It's tough to explain."

"Is that why you felt we couldn't talk about this?"

Gabe lifted a shoulder as he shook his head. "My mistake."

"Don't let it happen again," Jack said, pointing a finger. "Okay. I've got work to do."

"Me, too." Gabe looked at the envelope on his desk and picked it up. "Wait. These tickets were just delivered. It's for a fund-raiser next Saturday."

"You can't go?"

Gabe shook his head. "There are two tickets."

"So, find someone to use the other one."

"That's not going to happen," Gabe said. "It's at The Palms. Should be a young crowd. A good time."

Jack took the tickets and stuck them in his inside coat pocket. "If you're sure. I hate to see them go to waste." Then he walked to the office doorway, the floor of the portable shaking with every heavy footfall. "For crying out loud, this is a multimillion-dollar company. Can we please find permanent office space soon?"

And there was the heart of the problem, Gabe thought. He didn't want anything permanent. Ever again.

He hadn't told Jack about the "thing" with Rebecca. And it wasn't because he was worried that his friend would disapprove. Just the opposite. He was afraid Jack would say it was time to move on.

Rebecca sat on the rolling stool in the exam room and made some notes in Amy's chart. Based on the ultrasound and her best guess, the teen was starting her eighth month. But there was no way to be absolutely sure unless she could get more information. The more the better. A doctor could never have too much when treating a patient.

Rebecca swiveled the stool and met Amy's gaze. "Do you have any idea when the baby was conceived?"

The teen looked startled before indifference cloaked her expression. "No."

The curt answer was a clue to Rebecca that she wasn't telling the truth. She'd expected Amy to ask why she wanted to know, but Amy was still not participating in this pregnancy except with her body. She'd hoped that the sister/brother breakthrough in the hospital would make a difference. So far it wasn't showing. Unlike her baby.

"Do you want to talk about the father?" Rebecca asked.

"What's the point? He's a jerk."

The kind of jerk who'd dumped her for her best friend? Or the kind who'd assaulted her? The closed expression on her face gave nothing away.

"The point is that ignoring the obvious is counterproductive." She pulled some booklets from a display on the built-in desk and stood. "These pamphlets have a lot of good information that I'd like you to read."

Amy took the material. "What for?"

"You're in the third trimester of this pregnancy, Amy. It's time to get involved. The baby is almost fully formed. Soon it will be all about him—or her—gaining weight before the birth."

The teen set the booklets on the exam table beside her. "Whatever."

Not good enough, Rebecca thought.

"You need to start preparing to care for your baby."

"If you say so."

"I say so. And something else."

The teen exhaled loudly. "What?"

"I think it would be a good idea to contact your father."

All traces of bored indifference disappeared. "No way."

"He needs to know what's going on with his daughter."

"No, he doesn't. He's never cared."

Rebecca couldn't believe that. After all, the man had raised Gabe to be a caring man. She couldn't believe he'd been so indifferent toward his daughter. "Amy, he's your father—"

"And I'm the one he blames for killing my mother."

"I'm sure that's not true. He grieved for her, but—"

"He was never around," she snapped. "If he wasn't forced to get involved in my life, he ignored me. Hannah was the one who showed me how to do my hair. And when I got old enough she taught me about makeup."

And then Hannah died. Both Gabe and Amy had lost the woman who'd been so important to them, each in a different way. Then what? Amy acted out? Dated the wrong guys? Negative attention was better than none at all as she'd cried out for her father to notice her? Had she put herself in a situation she couldn't get out of? It was a very possible scenario, but there was no way to be sure unless the teen opened up. Moments ago she'd displayed more passion and emotion than Rebecca had ever seen. But now it was gone and the hostile teen was back.

"Okay. If you don't want your father involved, I won't push." For now, she added silently.

Amy only nodded.

Normally at this point she wanted to see her patients every other week, then once a week in the last month before birth. Everything was stable with Amy, but the feeling that this pregnancy was a ticking bomb wouldn't go away.

"I want to see you next week," Rebecca said.

"Why?"

She glanced up from the chart and attempted humor. "What? You don't like coming to see me?"

"It's not that. I just wondered—" Amy hesitated, then shrugged and said, "Okay."

"Stop and see Grace to make an appointment," Rebecca said.

Amy slid off the exam table and was out the door like a shot. Rebecca sat at the built-in desk and added some notes to her chart, then stood and walked past the exam table. She noticed the reading material Amy had left behind. She shook her head, frustrated that she couldn't help this troubled girl help herself. She grabbed the booklets and walked to the reception area, hoping to catch her before she left. Amy was nowhere in sight, but Gabe was just putting an appointment card into the pocket of his white dress shirt.

He smiled. "Hi."

"Hi."

The sight of him made her stomach pitch and roll. So much for hoping absence would make her heart idle in neutral. She'd last seen him two weeks ago when he'd told her that he would promise her anything if she kept staring at him the way she was. The thing was, she had no idea how she'd looked. It might have been a compliment. She thought he'd said she was pretty but she couldn't be sure. Especially since he'd apologized for kissing her. That hurt because it had meant a lot to her. The biggest problem was that she couldn't stay mad at him. That made it difficult to maintain her defenses.

Unfortunately, she needed to discuss with him what had just happened with Amy. "Gabe, do you have a minute?"

"Sure. Amy's waiting in the car." His shoulder lifted, a small movement that somehow conveyed his frustration. "As usual."

He disappeared from the reception window, then opened the door between the waiting room and exam areas before following her into her office.

She leaned back and half sat on the corner of her desk. "Have a seat."

"Why? Did something happen with Amy? Is she all right?"

"She's fine."

For the moment. At least one of the Thornes was curious and engaged in this situation.

"Then what did you want to talk about?"

"I thought you should know that I encouraged her to contact her father."

One eyebrow lifted. "Really?"

"It's not what you're thinking—"

"Since when are you a mind reader?"

"What do you mean?" she asked.

"How do you know what I'm thinking?"

"I just figured you went to the place where I was trying to talk her into going home."

"You figured wrong."

"So you're okay with her staying?"

"Yeah."

He sat in one of the chairs facing the desk, which put him squarely in her comfort zone. And just like that her zone was pretty uncomfortable.

"This is a big shift for you," she commented.

"Right back at you," he said.

"Well, she blew me off. But before that she let some stuff slip. She said your father blames her for your mother's death and never cared about her."

"Dad and I had a hard time after my mother died," he admitted, shifting in the chair. "He worked a lot, building the business into the multimillion-dollar company I took over. I kept busy so I wouldn't have to be home. There was football and classes. Studying." He met her gaze. "Most of my friends had mixed feelings about going away to college. I couldn't wait to get out of there. I had my pick of schools. The year my mother died, I got the highest grades ever."

She could relate. After her assault, she buried herself in studies and got a pretty impressive grade point average. "So, essentially, you lost your mother *and* father, and Amy never had much guidance at all."

He scratched his head thoughtfully. "When you put it like that it sounds pretty harsh. And I never thought about it that way. But I suppose there's some truth in it."

"Amy told me Hannah was the one who taught her about girl stuff."

"I knew Hannah had asked Amy to be her maid of honor at the wedding, but I guess I just thought she was doing it to be politically correct. Until that day in the hospital, I don't think I understood how much Amy missed her."

"And when she died, Amy was alone again."

"Yeah."

And like his sister's, his hooded expression gave no clue to his feelings. But she didn't need a clue. She already knew he'd lost the love of his life. But he'd left Texas to avoid painful memories leaving Amy alone to deal with her grief.

"Maybe the two of you need to talk about losing Hannah," she suggested. At his look she added, "She was important to both of you. It's a shared loss. Unlike the mother she never knew. She needs to know she can count on you, and reaching out would start the process. Think about it."

"I will." He stood and looked down at her, a thoughtful expression making him even more handsome and intriguing. "Tell me something, Doc, aren't you tired of my family?"

"No. Not if it will help Amy."

"Well, turnabout is fair play. Tell me about you."

That put a knot in her stomach, which effectively stopped the pitch and roll. She didn't like talking about herself. It started out with the basics then went to more personal questions, like why there was no one special. She wasn't going there. Her past was poison to a relationship. He'd kissed her, but that didn't give him a right to personal information.

"There's not much to tell."

"So tell me what there is. What was it like being smarter than everyone else? Your parents must have been proud."

She thought back. "I guess. Mostly they were clueless about what to do with a brainer geek who was bored in school."

"So what did they do?"

"At first they listened to the teachers who suggested skipping grades. Then they kind of stood back and let me do my thing."

"So you raised yourself?"

She thought about that. "Kind of. Yeah."

"For the record. You did a good job. You're a good doctor."

"Medicine is the easy part."

"Not for most people. You are exceptionally special," he said.

If he knew her secret, he'd know how big a lie that was. But there was no reason for him to know because there wasn't now, nor would there ever be, anything of a personal nature between them.

"Where are they?" he asked. "Your parents, I mean."

"In Southern California. Close enough for us to see each other often. They're both accountants."

"More comfortable with numbers than beautiful brainer geeks?"

"Yeah," she said, surprised that he was so intuitive. Then his words sank in. "No. I mean I'm not— You know—"

"Beautiful?" His blue eyes sparkled with wickedness.

"Yeah, that. I'm not."

"Yeah, that." He gently traced a finger down her nose. "You are."

He got that look in his eyes again, the one he got just before kissing her. Her body responded as if he'd just touched his lips to hers. Her insides turned to liquid and her heart pounded until she was sure he must hear or see it.

One of the benefits of a high IQ was never being at a loss for words. Except now. She had no idea what to say to him. Fortunately, he wasn't such a dweeb.

"Amy's waiting. I have to go." He tapped his pocket where he'd put the appointment card. "See you in a week. If not before."

And then he was gone. She sank into the chair that was still warm from his body and shivered as if he'd touched her. When her brain was firing on all cylinders again, two things bothered her. First, she'd talked about herself, a rule she hardly ever broke. Second, she'd forgotten to give him the reading material for his sister.

That wasn't like her. Both were symptoms of trouble. If it were science, she would know what to do. But it wasn't, and that scared her.

Chapter Seven

Gabe took Amy home after her appointment, then went back to the hospital to meet Jack and finish up his preparation for tomorrow's inspection. This was an important project, and no matter how distracted he'd been, failure wasn't an option.

It was now way past dinnertime and he was suddenly starving. The cafeteria was open, but choices were limited because it was late. The only thing he could get was a wilted salad or a burger that could double as a hockey puck. He picked the puck and paid for it, then took his plastic tray and rounded the corner to the fountain drink dispensers.

After getting an iced tea, he scanned the sparsely occupied room looking for Jack. He found him in the center where he could check out people, meaning nurse-type people, walking to and from the elevator just outside the room.

"You're incorrigible," Gabe said, setting his tray down.

"What?" he asked, feigning innocence.

"Hey. This is me, remember?"

Jack grinned. "I like women, my friend. I like everything about them. The way they look, smell, walk and talk. I like watching them. So sue me."

Actually, he envied his friend. Jack had a social life and he knew how to use it. He was a notorious flirt and proud of it. Gabe had a life but wasn't using it for much of anything. Lately, he'd felt a vague dissatisfaction about that. He was getting used to having Amy around. In spite of that, he felt a more acute loneliness than he'd experienced even after Hannah died. And he was pretty sure it was all about Rebecca.

Gabe took a bite out of his burger and chewed thoughtfully. "It wasn't a criticism, my friend. Just an observation."

"That sounded brooding. How's that working for you?"

"It's not. Which is just the way I want it." Gabe heard the edge to his voice.

"This is me, remember?" Jack said, apparently unfazed. "I loved Hannah, too, but it's time—"

"Don't go there," Gabe said. "I'm not interested in dating."

"Okay." Jack put up a hand touching the other palm to his fingers in a *T* for time out. "I just hate to see you going through the motions. You're living, but not really living, you know?"

He knew. "Look, Jack, I—" He stopped when Rebecca stepped out of the elevator and headed for the cafeteria.

"What?" Jack said, staring at him, then glancing in the same direction. "Holy Mother of God."

"Back off, Jack."

"You know her?" His friend made no attempt to hide the surprise in his voice.

"She's my sister's doctor."

Rebecca was just coming into the cafeteria when she

spotted him and did a double take. She hesitated, then walked over to the table. "Hello, Gabe."

"Hi." When Jack loudly cleared his throat, Gabe said, "This is my partner, Jackson O'Neill."

"That's O'Neill with two *L*s," Jack said, extending his hand. Rebecca took it and smiled. "Nice to meet you."

"What are you doing here?" Gabe asked, then winced at the lame question. That's what happened when you didn't use your social life. Communication skills got rusty. And since when had he started caring about that sort of thing?

"This is where I work," she answered wryly.

"I knew that."

"One of my patients is in labor," she explained. "I just wanted to grab a quick bite while I can. It's late. What are you doing here?"

"I'm building a hospital expansion."

"I knew that," she said. "But it's pretty late. I thought you were more of a nine-to-five guy."

"The building inspector is coming tomorrow, and we want to be sure everything is ready," Jack said.

"This is a different type of project for the company," Gabe added.

"Why?" she asked.

"Because it's a hospital, not a hotel," Gabe said. Being a doctor, she probably already knew this, but he added, "It's specialized construction. We have to put in pipes for oxygen, carbon dioxide and nitrous. Those pipes have to be leak tested and certified before we can close up the walls. The electrical is more complicated because of monitor wires and plugs for emergency power. Every room not only has to be fireproof, it's critical that dampers shut down and keep smoke from the ventilation system."

"I see."

"And this is our first project in Las Vegas. Very visible. Our reputation in this town is on the line. We want the inspection to go off without a hitch."

"Not only that, he's a little obsessed with work," Jack explained. "I've been trying to slow him down to warp speed, but so far without success."

"Good luck with that. And the inspection tomorrow." She glanced between them. "Nice to see you, Gabe."

"You, too."

She moved away and he stared after her, savoring the seductive scent of her skin, watching the sway of her hips, the slender column of her neck, the way the unflattering fluorescent lighting turned her hair into a golden halo. Jack was right about women. But this woman in particular did something to him. And just like that he wasn't brooding anymore. Just moments in a room with her and his mood went from zero to off the scale.

He didn't like it. Today she lifted his spirits, tomorrow his heart, and that was bad. If it were a disease, he could take medicine, but there was no treatment he knew of to stop this disorder, no indicators that would show up on an ultrasound or any other sophisticated machine. Maybe she was right that medicine was the easy part. Because this was damned hard. But he could no longer ignore the fact that she was a desirable woman he couldn't stop thinking about. The realization twisted him up inside.

"Earth to Gabe."

"What?" He met his friend's gaze.

"Why didn't you tell me Amy's doctor was such a babe?"

"Because it didn't seem relevant. She's good at what she does and that's the important thing."

"Rebecca—" Jack waved her over. "Why don't you join us."

She hesitated. "I don't want to intrude. Besides, I don't have much time."

"Neither does Gabe. Keep him company while I run up to the fourth floor and check on the electrical. You can meet me there, buddy."

Rebecca looked uncomfortable as she set her tray down. "I don't want to chase you off."

"You're not." As he walked away, Jack opened his coat to find a pen, then turned back. He pulled something from his inside jacket pocket. "I just remembered, Gabe, I've got plans Saturday night. I can't use these tickets."

"Jack, I—"

"Take Rebecca." He dropped the envelope on the table between them. "Gotta go."

They both stared at the tickets, then looked at each other. Gabe didn't know what to say. There was a time when he could have smoothed over something like this without missing a beat. But he was out of practice, and if not for Jack, it wouldn't be necessary to flex those muscles now.

"You've known him a long time?" Rebecca asked, almost as if she could read his thoughts.

"Since we were ten."

"Ah." She nodded, then took a bite of salad.

"He's not subtle," Gabe commented.

"Not very, no." She met his gaze. "Does he try to fix you up often?"

"No."

In fact never. Until now. Jack had always understood him. Until now. But his friend didn't understand what Gabe had been through. If he did, he'd know that advice to "move forward" was easier to hand out than it was to take.

"This is awkward."

Lifting a shoulder, she said, "Don't worry about it."

Gabe ate the rest of his burger without really tasting it,

which was a blessing. Then he looked at her. "I don't suppose you'd be interested—"

She shook her head. "Not a good idea."

That's for sure. Note to self, he thought. Get even with Jack.

"So who's having a baby?" he asked. "Anyone I know?"

"I don't think so. And even if you did, I couldn't tell you. There are those pesky privacy laws," she said.

"You're such a rule follower."

"So says mister Type A personality."

"What was your first clue?"

Her brown eyes warmed with challenge. "You wouldn't be here making sure everything's going according to plans, and codes, and specs, oh my."

"Okay, smart aleck. Chalk up one for you."

"Thank you." She twisted the plastic cap from her bottle of water and took a drink.

She pressed her lips together to remove the moisture and the movement twisted up his insides in an entirely different way, a way that had nothing to do with his conflicted feelings and everything to do with lust. A pure and simple yearning to hold her, kiss her until she was fire in his arms, then make love to her.

He *wanted* this woman.

It didn't make him happy, but he could no longer ignore the fact, either. Apparently, Jack had noticed, too. Gabe could live with this change as long as he didn't cross the line between wanting her and needing her.

He picked up the envelope and started to stick the tickets into the inside pocket of his jacket. "I'm sorry Jack made you uncomfortable. There will be swift and sure retribution."

She smiled as he'd hoped she would. "Don't hurt him. Or don't tell me about it. There's this little thing called the Hippocratic oath we doctors take before we can practice medicine. One of the most basic things is to do no harm. I'm quite sure knowledge of premeditated harm would require intervention on my part."

"Okay. I won't tell you. Obviously, Jack didn't think through that move. But please don't feel obligated. I don't mind going alone."

He was used to it. T&O Construction contributed to several charities. But this particular cause was a first for them.

"So you're still going?" she asked.

He nodded. "I'll make an appearance. Participate in the silent auction, then duck out as quickly as possible. All proceeds go to the Southern Nevada Rape Crisis Center."

Rebecca was taking a drink of water and started to cough. Gabe patted her back until she stopped. "You okay?"

She nodded. "I swallowed wrong."

"I hate when that happens."

"How did the company happen to get involved in this particular benefit?" she asked, almost too casually.

He shrugged. "We got a call from one of the local TV news anchors. This is the third annual Nora's Night on the Town. We have a budget for contributions and it's an opportunity to network."

"It's also a worthy cause."

Gabe might have turned down the request if Rebecca hadn't suggested that Amy could possibly be a victim. She hadn't opened up about that and he wouldn't push the issue. But when he'd gotten the call, he remembered and agreed to participate.

"Yeah, it is a worthy cause."

With an odd expression on her face, she met his gaze. "On second thought, I'd like to go with you. If the invitation is still open."

"Okay." He nodded. "Good."

Her pager went off and she looked at it. "I have to go."

"Right. I'll call you."

She nodded, smiled and hurried away.

And just like that he had a date. A few minutes ago he had the sensation of get-it-on-get-it-over-with lust. It was easy to understand. He was a guy. He wanted her, but he also liked her.

And that was the part that made everything so complicated.

Rebecca stared at her reflection in her mirrored closet door and wondered if Gabe would notice any difference. It wasn't scrubs or a white lab coat, but... A few days wasn't much notice for an event that was getting a whole lot of local news coverage. Right after agreeing to go, panic had set in because she didn't want to embarrass him. What did one wear to a high-profile benefit?

A quick trip to Fashion Show Mall had been fruitless. She'd found one dress guaranteed to make his eyes pop out, but it cost enough to inoculate the children of a third-world country and was therefore not in her budget. Then she'd tried very hard to make herself believe she didn't care. Her old dress would be fine. But panic set in again when she realized she *did* care how she looked.

Grace came to the rescue. They were about the same size, and one of her dresses actually worked. It was black—always a good choice. The just-this-side-of-safe neckline was held up by thin straps and showed just a hint of cleavage, and the column skirt hit her just above the knee. What had seemed perfect that morning in the light of day now didn't cover nearly enough skin. Her satin pumps were good and the black crystal chandelier earrings just enough jewelry.

Grace had pronounced her "hot." Rebecca thought she looked okay, but wished with all her heart she wasn't so fashion challenged. More important—what the hell had she been thinking?

She'd told Gabe no. *N-O*. He'd been fine with that—almost

seemed relieved, and the awkward moment was successfully sidestepped. And then he'd mentioned the cause behind the event—a center that would help sexual assault victims. Her heart had skipped. Her pulse had raced. And blood flow to her brain must have been interrupted just long enough, because the words "On second thought I'd like to go with you" came out of her mouth. She wouldn't have blamed Gabe for thinking she was crazy, but he'd said okay.

Facing an evening with him was much like her dilemma of what to wear. She wanted to believe she didn't care. But as she waited for him to pick her up, panic was settling in because she was afraid she cared too much. On top of that, it was difficult for her to welcome a man into her personal space.

How she wished he was a little less a gentleman and would have agreed to her suggestion to meet at The Palms. Public equaled safe. But he'd insisted on picking her up. Checking the clock on the nightstand beside her bed, she calculated fifteen minutes to spare. Time enough to put her key, credit card, cash and identification into her evening bag. When Gabe arrived she would be wearing her wrap, and after opening the door they would simply walk out. Problem solved.

As she was going downstairs, her phone rang. When she answered, it was Gabe at the security gate and she had no choice but to buzz him through. He would be there in less than a minute. Before she had time to do more than pull her wrap out of the closet, the doorbell rang.

She looked through the peephole and could clearly see him in the porch light. Not only was he a gentleman, he was early. What was that about?

Taking a deep breath, she unlocked the dead bolt and opened the door. "Hi," she said brightly. Too brightly. She sounded like a perky idiot.

"Hi."

The peephole hadn't done him justice! The event was black tie optional and he'd taken the option. In his traditional black tux with crisp white shirt, he looked incredibly handsome and sophisticated. And she was so out of her league.

She glanced down and smoothed her skirt when she noticed he was staring at her. "Is something wrong? The dress isn't right. I knew it—"

He reached over and touched a finger to her lips to silence her. "You look beautiful."

Was it her imagination or did his voice sound just a bit huskier than usual?

"I didn't know what to wear. This is actually Grace's dress. She let me borrow it. I've never been to one of these benefits, and it was such short notice. I hope I look okay. You guys have it easy. A tux is a tux. But dresses can be too casual, too dressy. Too—" The amused expression on his face stopped her. "I'm babbling."

"Most charmingly."

"Oh, please."

"I don't think you're the fishing-for-compliments type. And I'm not the kind of guy who says something he doesn't mean. So, one more time. You look beautiful. In fact, you take my breath away. Believe it."

"Okay."

They stared at each other for several moments and he said, "Are you ready to go?"

She wished. This was the moment she'd hoped to avoid by being prepared to walk right out the door. He was so dashing, so sexy, and she'd never wished more to be normal than she did at this moment. In a normal world she wouldn't give a thought to inviting a man into her home. It only took that one time and the subsequent betrayal and violation that followed to change her forever.

"I...I'll be ready to go in a second. I just have to throw some things in my evening bag."

"Rebecca—"

"What?"

He looked down and blew out a long breath, then met her gaze. "I just want to apologize."

"For what?" she asked.

"I haven't been out with anyone since—" He stopped, and the muscle in his jaw jerked. "Since before Hannah. It's been a very long time for me and I'm rusty."

"That's okay."

"No. It's not. Hell of a time to think of this, but I should have brought flowers. A corsage. Something. Right?"

"I am so not the right person to ask."

That's when she realized he was still standing on the porch because she hadn't invited him inside. She stepped back and pulled the door wide. "Please come in. I'll just be a minute."

"Thanks." He followed her inside and looked around. "Nice place. Good location, too."

She lived in the Inspiration Point condo complex off Paseo Verde between Green Valley Ranch Parkway and Pecos Road.

"I like it here. Not far from my office and The District is just down the street."

"I hear it has great shopping and restaurants."

"I hear that, too."

"You haven't been there?" he asked, surprised.

She shook her head. "I don't go out much, either."

"I find that hard to believe," he said, sliding his hands into the pockets of his tuxedo pants.

"I'm a busy doctor."

"You're also a beautiful woman."

What did she say to that? God she hated being a geek. One could never go wrong being polite. "Thank you."

"You don't have to thank me. I had nothing to do with it."

"But it's nice of you to say so," she amended.

"Stating the obvious isn't nice. Just the truth."

"Would you like a tour of the place?" she asked, suddenly eager to take the attention off herself.

"Yes," he said.

"I liked the open concept. This is the great room with fireplace. The kitchen is there," she said, leading him farther inside.

"Nice fireplace. The black granite in the kitchen is really dramatic with the white cupboards, too."

"Yeah. It's one of the things that sold me on the place. And the view." The whole back of the condo was sliding glass doors and windows that showed off the lights from The Strip.

"What's upstairs?"

"Three bedrooms and a loft. And more view from the master bedroom."

"Sounds nice," he said, still looking around. "How long have you been here?"

"Not long." She followed his gaze to the stack of boxes in the corner and said, "I'm still unpacking."

"I can see that." He looked at his watch. "We should probably get going."

She'd been on guard for an invitation to see her upstairs and was surprised when he suggested leaving. Good to know they were on the same page. Although, the fact that he didn't ask was more disappointing than she would have thought. In fact, he was nothing like she'd expected.

She'd been braced for aggressive behavior. He was so charmingly uncomfortable, so refreshingly honest, that he put her at ease. It was both good news and bad.

"Right. Let me just get my things." Her purse was sitting on the window seat in the entryway and she quickly grabbed the essentials. Then she slid her black shawl over her shoulders and said, "I'm ready."

"Okay."

Gabe opened the door and let her precede him outside where she turned and locked up. Then he took her hand and settled her fingers into the bend of his elbow as he walked her down the several steps to where his silver car waited at the curb.

For the first time since Grace had said it, Rebecca felt hot. All over. And it had nothing to do with the way she looked. It was all about how Gabe made her feel. This must be what it was like to be the prom queen who had a date with the most popular guy at school.

She was grateful they were leaving, but not for the reason she would have expected.

It was herself she didn't trust.

Chapter Eight

It wasn't often Rebecca was a passenger and could enjoy the lights on the Las Vegas Strip. She loved the way the castle turrets of the Excalibur were lit up. And Paris's Eiffel Tower. And the elegance of Bellagio. After driving north on the 15 Freeway, Gabe exited at Flamingo Road and turned left, passing the Rio before turning left into The Palms Hotel. The BMW's smooth ride didn't hide its harnessed power and somehow that increased the level of her excitement. She would have preferred canceling altogether before Gabe had confessed his nervousness, and she upgraded her present condition from critical to guarded. She was out with a man and so far it wasn't awful.

They pulled up to the valet, left the car in good hands, then walked inside, assaulted by the sound of ringing slot machines and the buzz of voices. Following the wooden floor in a circle, they spotted the signs directing everyone to the event, then took the elevator up to the appropriate floor. After checking in at the registration desk, they joined the crowd already gathered for the benefit. Gabe took two flutes of champagne from the tray of a passing waiter and handed one to her.

He held up his glass. "What should we drink to?"

Before she could answer let's drink to geeks gone wild, microphone static and a call for attention drowned out conversation. Everyone turned to an area at the front of the room where a fortyish woman in a floor-length royal-blue gown stood.

"Welcome. I'm Trish Kendrick, Director of the Southern Nevada Rape Crisis Foundation, an organization committed to helping those touched by sexual violence to heal from the trauma." Vigorous applause followed and when it waned she continued. "We know there are many worthy causes in need of your support and we are incredibly grateful that you chose us.

"Thanks to your generosity we can continue to fund many worthwhile programs." Trish put her hands together and clapped as she let her glance scan the whole room. "We're dedicated to assisting victims and their families, but education is the key to creating a community free of violence where all of us can live without fear."

Cheers and enthusiastic applause erupted when she paused. Trish nodded her approval. "Some of our education programs are presentations to age-appropriate high school students. Too many are under the impression that this crime is perpetrated by a stranger jumping out of the shadows. Unfortunately that happens, but over half of the people attacked are acquainted with their attacker. Teens and college age students often experience the violence. And we need to get the message out. Don't keep rape a secret. And you are not alone."

Rebecca looked up at Gabe and saw the intense, angry expression that made the muscle in his jaw jerk. She knew he was thinking about Amy and her own suspicions about how the baby was conceived. How she hoped she was wrong.

Trish continued, "Our educational programs include guidelines on something as simple as what *yes, no* and *maybe* mean. But there's no maybe about my gratitude. Thank you for coming. Have a wonderful evening. And don't forget to visit the room next door where items are on display for the silent auction."

Rebecca was lost in her own thoughts as the applause decreased, then faded away. A sensation of sadness slid over her. The violence she'd experienced had been so incredibly personal, intimate and vile and she'd done everything wrong. She'd kept it a secret and handled the consequences alone.

"Rebecca?"

She looked up. "I'm sorry. Did you say something?"

"Are you all right?"

"Of course. Why?"

"You look like you just saw a ghost."

Ghosts of the trauma that would never go away. She tried to smile. "It's nothing."

"Were you thinking about Amy?"

She nodded, glad she didn't have to lie. But she'd also been thinking about herself. Then something occurred to her. "Did you buy tickets to this fund-raiser because of what I said about my suspicions?"

"It tipped the scales," he admitted.

"The center is there for family members, too. I don't know that I'm right about your sister, but clearly she doesn't want to talk about how this pregnancy happened. And it's probably not a good idea to force the issue. You might want to contact them for counseling on how to deal with the situation."

"I might just do that." He held his glass up again. "Let's drink to communication."

"Good idea." She smiled, then tapped her glass to his.

"Let's go check out what's up for auction so I can spend some more money."

"I would be very happy to help spend your money."

"Excellent."

They moved through the crowd, and Rebecca felt his hand at the small of her back, guiding and protective. It was courteous, thoughtful, qualities of a man well brought up. His mother would be proud. That didn't come close to describing Rebecca's feelings. The touch sent shivers of awareness over her skin, making her tremble.

Gabe looked down. "Are you cold?"

"I'm fine," she lied.

After waiting in a short line, they made it inside the room and wandered past several tables displaying items donated by local businesses and individuals. There was jewelry, spa packages, hotel stays, paintings and blown glass contributed by a prestigious gallery.

Rebecca stopped to admire a porcelain figure titled "Woman." The sign also said suggested bids started at a thousand dollars. "This is really beautiful."

"It is," he agreed.

But when Rebecca glanced up, he wasn't looking at the figurine. He was staring at her with a sort of painful intensity that made her heart race.

"We're holding up the line," she said, wishing that she was more witty, glib and entertaining. This was on-the-job training, practice in the field and maybe next time she would handle it without turning into the crowd control police.

Rebecca had always been busy with classes and studying and skipping grades in school. She'd never acted like a schoolgirl when she was one, but probably this awkwardness is what it would have felt like. Now she was too old for it, and falling on her face.

Maybe if her parents had known how to guide their gifted daughter, things would have been different. Maybe if someone had advised her to slow down and savor the moment instead of worrying that she wasn't doing justice to her high IQ she might have learned to be comfortable in her own skin. But now her skin was hyperaware every time she brushed against Gabe. When he casually put his arm around her, she wanted to giggle and sigh and tremble like that schoolgirl she'd never been and indulge this attraction that just kept growing.

And her reaction proved the old saying. "You could dress the dweeb up, but you couldn't take her anywhere." Not if you wanted to have a good time.

Except, Gabe wasn't after a good time. He hadn't asked her here. Not exactly. Jack had practically shamed him into it. Something she would do well to remember.

"Hold on," he said. He took a piece of paper from the table and wrote on it, then put it in the box provided.

She blinked. "You made a bid?"

"Yes."

"More than the minimum?"

"Oh, yeah."

Of course. Because millionaires could do that. But millionaires were also human. No matter how much it seemed that guys like him were perfect, she knew that wasn't so. He was a golden boy with a broken heart. And he'd said it would never heal. It was a bitter pill for a healer to swallow, but the woman in her would be wise to heed the warning.

The evening progressed with dinner and dessert. Afterward, the results of the silent auction were announced and Gabe's bid had been accepted. He made arrangements to have the figurine delivered to his home, then they got to the dancing portion of the evening. A dj took over the microphone and played a variety of up-tempo songs that by silent agreement they ignored. Then the slow, smoky strains of a ballad began.

Gabe sighed. "I haven't done this for a really long time, but if you'd like to dance, I'm game."

He was leaving her an out. If she were smart, she'd take it. "I'd like that."

Apparently she wasn't as smart as everyone thought. But this was about wanting more than anything to have an acceptable excuse to be close to him, spend time with him.

As they made their way to the floor in the center of the room, he did the hand at the back thing. Then she turned and he took her in his arms and settled her securely against him. It was quite a lovely place to be, and she wanted to snuggle into the warmth and sigh with contentment. Instead she concentrated on following his lead, stumbling only once or twice.

The second time, she looked up wryly. "Just so you know this is not the fault of any educational institution I attended. I learned the basics, and that's about it."

"You're doing fine."

"No. You're doing fine. I'm just along for the ride."

And loving it more than she should.

"Speaking of riding along, why did you change your mind about coming tonight?"

The question startled her, making her stumble again, but his strong arms steadied her. She couldn't tell him it was because she was curious about the available support for victims of attacks like the one she'd experienced. That would be revealed on a need-to-know basis, and a serious relationship was the only reason he would need to know. That wasn't going to happen.

Gabe had taken some horrible emotional hits and flat-out said he didn't want to care again. Neither did she. The fact was, if this benefit wasn't for a cause close to her heart, she wouldn't be close to Gabe. She would have turned down his halfhearted invitation.

"I don't think I can put into words why I changed my mind. I guess it just comes under the heading 'seemed like a good idea at the time.'"

He pulled her just a little closer. "Well, I'm glad you did."

Just like that, so was she. And therein was the problem. She didn't want to be in a place where she had to take a risk again. She didn't want to confide her own violation and the violence she'd experienced. She didn't want...

Whoa. Time out. As usual, she was making things far more complicated than necessary. This was one night, for a good cause and she was making it into a bare-your-soul experience. He had two tickets and she was available. End of story. There was no reason to borrow trouble.

There wasn't now, nor would there ever be, a reason for her to tell him what had happened to her.

About five minutes after leaving The Palms, conversation from the right-hand seat had ceased. Of course the fact that it was midnight could have something to do with that. Gabe looked over to see Cinderella leaning back with her eyes closed. Either Rebecca was avoiding conversation or she was worn out. Or both. It didn't matter, really, but he couldn't help being curious. She'd been different tonight. The wary woman he normally saw when he was with her had eventually disappeared. In her place was a fun lady doctor with a wicked sense of humor and a way with a waltz.

He glanced over again and couldn't help smiling. She looked comfortable. Relaxed. And so beautiful the sight of her made his chest hurt. But that wasn't why he was glad she'd come with him. He'd missed having someone in that passenger seat. Someone not his sister.

Gabe made the transition from the 15 South to the 215 Beltway East, toward Henderson. Rebecca was still asleep and started a little, sighing softly. The sound seared through him, stirring up lust. At the same time a feeling of tenderness took hold and squeezed.

When he'd extended the invitation for the benefit, he was relieved when she'd turned him down, decided it was for the best. And he wasn't sure what had made Rebecca change her mind about coming with him tonight. It was right after he'd told her what the benefit was for.

When he'd picked her up at her condo, it had not looked at all promising for a positive outcome to the evening. He hadn't done this in a really long time, and she'd acted as if she expected him to put her up against the wall and shoot her. After he'd confessed his nerves, her attitude relaxed, softened somehow. It was as if he'd passed some kind of test.

Now she was sitting beside him. He liked having her there. He liked *her*.

After exiting the Beltway, he turned right on Green Valley Parkway, then right again on Paseo Verde and passed The District and Green Valley Ranch Resort before turning left into Rebecca's complex. When he came to the closed gates, he was glad she'd told him that the last four digits of her home number were her gate code because he didn't have to wake her to get them inside. All too soon he pulled up in front of her place and turned off the ignition.

He expected her to wake, but she didn't. In fact she was sleeping pretty deeply. Apparently, a couple of late-night deliveries and the unforgiving pace of a doctor's life were taking a toll. If anyone deserved some rest, it was the special lady who helped life happen.

Maybe he could get her inside without waking her. He picked up her purse and took her key, then quietly let himself out of the car and unlocked her front door. Gently he opened the passenger door and undid her seat belt. Very carefully, he slid one arm behind her back and the other beneath her legs and checked to make sure he hadn't disturbed her. The street-light drew his attention to the dark sweep of her long lashes, the curve of her cheek, the fullness of her lips. Something tightened inside him, something rusty and unfamiliar, but so compelling and intense that adrenaline surged through him.

He wanted to kiss her. Maybe if he didn't know that she tasted like heaven, he could have resisted. But he'd already made that mistake once; now resisting temptation turned painful. He needed the touch more than his next breath.

Gabe lowered his mouth to hers, deliberately keeping the contact soft, hardly more than a brush of butterfly wings. Instantly he felt her tense just before he heard her gasp. He lifted his head and saw that her eyes were wide and scared.

"No." She put her hands flat against his chest and pushed. "Get off me. Let me go!"

"Rebecca, it's okay. It's me. Gabe."

"Let me go."

Was she still asleep? Having a bad dream? "Wake up, Rebecca—"

"Don't touch me—" Panic laced her voice. "Get your hands off."

He did, but everything in him wanted to gather her in his arms and reassure her that she was safe. That he would never hurt her.

He made his voice as calm as possible when he said, "Rebecca, it's Gabe. We went out tonight. Remember? You're in my car. In front of your house. You're home."

Not sure whether or not she was awake, he squatted beside her because he sensed that looming over her would be more frightening.

Her breathing was harsh, frantic and her chest rose and fell rapidly. The same streetlights that moments ago had high-lighted her beauty now exposed the fear. He hated that she was afraid of him.

She shrank back, away from him, and her gaze darted from his face to her front door as if she were calculating her chances of successful escape. She drew in air as she touched a trembling hand to her forehead.

"Gabe—"

"I'm here." Thank God she recognized him.

"I…I guess I fell asleep."

"Yeah."

But this was so much more than her being disoriented after waking from a deep sleep. He felt it in his gut that this was way more than a bad dream.

He held a hand out. "I'll take you inside."

Her gaze locked on his and shame mixed with alarm. She glanced around. "My purse—"

"It's inside," he assured her. "I used your key to unlock the door. I only wanted to let you sleep a little longer."

"Oh. I…I don't know what to say."

"You don't have to say anything." Not right now. But they would talk about this.

"I want to get out." She sat there, struggling to get her breathing under control as she watched and waited for him to give her space.

Gabe stood and backed away. "Okay."

She slid out of the car and rested her hand on the door for a second, steadying herself. He let her because he was afraid to touch her, afraid she would shatter. She gathered her composure for several moments without looking at him. And when she did, she couldn't manage a smile. "Thank you for taking me," she said, trying to follow the rules in spite of everything.

"Let's go in," he said.

"No." She seemed to sense the sharpness of her tone and looked at him. "That's okay. It's late."

"Rebecca, I— At least let me see you to the door."

"Please, just let me go in," she pleaded.

Grimly he nodded. "All right."

"Good night," she said.

It had been. Until now. He watched her walk inside and shut the door without looking at him.

For a long time he stood there but couldn't manage to make sense of what just happened. All he knew for sure was that the doc had issues. If anyone knew about issues, it was him. After losing first Hannah, then the baby within a week of each other, he would admit to personal wounds. Rebecca hid behind a facade of professionalism, but he knew there was something wounded in her, too.

He hadn't asked to start feeling again, but somehow it had happened. And he wasn't sure it was a good thing. In fact, there was only one thing he *was* sure of.

She'd managed to touch him, deep inside where no one had for a long time. When he'd touched her back, she'd been afraid of him. He couldn't stand that. He hated the fear he'd seen in Rebecca's eyes.

The question was, What was he going to do about it?

Chapter Nine

It had been a week, and Rebecca hadn't seen Gabe since the night she'd—well—she'd treated him a lot like a criminal. It wasn't her fault. She knew that. She'd been startled, and that horrible memory was always in her subconscious. It reared its ugly head at unexpected times. The blame for that ugly memory sat squarely with the man who'd forced himself on her. When she'd awakened from a deep sleep to find a man holding her, looming over her, she'd gone straight back to the bad place and panicked. And Gabe had paid the price for what another man had done to her.

In the years since the assault, she'd learned that though there was no shame, unfortunately there was no trust, either. Ten years and the bastard was still taking from her. She had a profession that she loved, but he'd stolen so much from her, including a personal life. No doubt Gabe thought she was a raving lunatic.

In the past seven days she'd spent far too much time and energy thinking about this because there never was going to be anything between her and Gabe. No one in Vegas would ever have bet on the two of them being a couple. But she couldn't seem to get it, or him, out of her mind. Maybe when she saw him, got the first post-meltdown, face-to-face meeting over with, she'd be able to stop thinking about him.

And that meeting would be soon. Amy was here in the office, the last appointment of the day, and Gabe hadn't missed one yet.

Rebecca lifted the chart from the holder on the outside of the exam room door. Before she saw a patient, the nurse would already have taken her blood pressure and weight and checked the glucose in the patient's sample.

Rebecca noted all Amy's numbers were within normal limits. She took a deep breath and opened the door, but bracing herself had been a waste of time. Amy was alone. Her brother wasn't in the room.

"Hi, Amy."

"Hi." Amy did a double take. "You look weird."

"I'm fine," Rebecca said with far more enthusiasm than she felt.

She'd been dreading seeing Gabe and had no idea how much she'd actually wanted to see him until she didn't see him. She shook her head to clear it. His sister was her patient, and that was the most important thing. "So, Amy, what's up?"

The teen shrugged.

"Your weight looks good. How are you feeling?"

"Okay, I guess."

"You guess? Any specific complaints?"

"I wake up every two hours to pee."

"That's normal. Other than that how are you sleeping?"

Amy rocked her hand back and forth in a so-so gesture. She put her hands on her belly. "I can't get comfortable."

"That's normal, too. I like to think it's Mother Nature's way of getting you ready to take care of your baby when it gets here. Babies need to eat frequently. That means he, or she, is going to wake up during the night."

Amy looked away, clearly not wanting to talk about caring for the baby. With approximately five weeks until she delivered, there wasn't much time left to work on winning her cooperation. Rebecca had hoped the teen would come around by now. Very soon she was going to be responsible for the welfare of a child. Or make a serious decision.

Rebecca was really getting worried about what would happen when the baby arrived. It wasn't just Amy's life she was concerned about. There was a child at risk, too.

"You're going to need help, Amy," Rebecca said gently.

"Gabe will help."

Rebecca remembered the strained expression on his face when he'd looked in Mercy Medical's newborn nursery. Her guess would be that he didn't have a lot of experience with infants.

"I'm sure your brother will do whatever he can. But does he know about babies?"

"Gabe can do anything," Amy said.

Not according to him, Rebecca thought. He didn't think he was the right person to help his sister through this but he'd stepped up as best he could. Somehow they needed to convince this traumatized girl to *want* to take care of her baby.

"The point is, do you know how to care for an infant?" Rebecca asked.

The question was direct and she didn't mean to be unkind, but the deadline was quickly approaching and facts needed to be faced.

"Are we done?" Amy started to slide off the exam table.

"No." Rebecca put her hand on the girl's shoulder, indicating she should lie on her back. "I need to check the baby."

The teen did as requested, but not without eye rolling and a long-suffering sigh. Rebecca put her stethoscope on Amy's belly and moved it around, listening for the fetus's heart rate, which was strong. "The baby sounds good."

Then she examined Amy's ankles and calves for edema, which was moderate, not uncommon at this stage of pregnancy. "Your legs are a little swollen. I want you to avoid salty foods and put the salt shaker away. It makes you retain fluid."

"Is that it?"

Rebecca held out her hand and assisted the girl to a sitting position. "For now. I'll see you next week."

"Okay." Amy slid off the table and headed for the door.

Rebecca followed, to make certain Amy made an appointment, she told herself. As they approached the front office, voices drifted to them—one was Grace. The other was male and it didn't sound like Gabe. Amy walked through the door, and Rebecca joined Grace at the reception window where she was talking with Jack O'Neill.

"I know your type," Grace said.

He leaned an elbow on the counter, the movement blatantly flirty and a clear invasion of space. "And what type would that be?"

"The type who is self-absorbed and egotistical."

He winced and put a hand over his heart. "I can't believe you said that."

"But I'm right, aren't I?"

"Pretty much," he said.

Grace laughed. "At least you're an honest scoundrel."

"Does it say somewhere that scoundrels are dishonest by

definition?" His wicked smile widened when he saw Rebecca. "Hey. Nice to see you again."

"You, too," she lied.

It wasn't exactly a lie. Jack was all right. He just wasn't Gabe. She knew by the way her heart jumped into her throat, then thudded when it hit bottom again that it was a symptom and she was in a lot of trouble.

"What are you doing here?" she asked.

"Gabe sent me to pick up Amy," he explained. He looked at the teen and draped an arm across her shoulders. "Hey, squirt. Everything okay?"

"Yeah."

"Grace, will you give Amy an appointment for a week from today?" Rebecca asked.

"Okay." The receptionist typed in the commands and pulled up the schedule. "How about the same time?" she asked, looking at the girl.

"I guess."

"Done." Grace handed her a card with the time and date written on it.

"Okay." Jack looked at Rebecca. "Did you have a good time at the benefit?"

It had been too much to hope he wouldn't bring that up. Especially since he'd been responsible for pushing her and Gabe together in the first place. Had he asked Gabe how it went? Had Gabe mentioned that she was a lunatic? She had no way of knowing. There had been no communication since the night in question.

"I had a great time," she said. That was the truth. Everything had been magical until the end.

It took every ounce of willpower she possessed, but she refrained from asking what Gabe thought of her. She was a grown woman. This wasn't junior high.

"Good." Jack looked at Amy. "Let's get you home, kiddo."

When she nodded, he looked at her, then winked at Grace. "Don't let the scoundrels get you down."

The outside door closed behind them, and Rebecca walked over to lock it. Amy was their last patient of the day.

"So you've met him before?" Grace asked.

"Jack?" Grace nodded and she said, "He's a friend of Gabe and Amy's from Texas."

"You could have warned me about Mr. Slick."

"I had no idea he would be here instead of—"

"Gabe?" Grace guessed.

"Yeah." She shrugged.

It was for the best. No harm, no foul, Rebecca thought.

"Did you know that Jack is an outrageous flirt?" Grace asked, leaning back in her chair with her arms folded over her chest.

"You're asking the wrong person. Social skills are not my specialty. Although I had a feeling."

"In the future, a flirt alert would be helpful."

"You can count on it. If there is a next time," she said.

There wouldn't be, at least for her and Gabe. Rebecca went to her office and closed the door. Leaning back against it she blew out a long breath. He hadn't missed a single appointment until after the night she'd gone mental on him. It didn't take superior social skills to understand the rejection. And the cut was far more than a superficial sting. She felt the rebuff as deeply as if he'd said she was too much trouble to deal with.

So much for no harm. This was a definite foul, and it hurt a lot.

After making her evening rounds to check on a couple of patients, Rebecca exited the hospital elevator on the first floor. She turned to her right and walked down the long hall, past the bank of employee lockers and out the back door to the doctor's parking lot. It was time to go home and she wasn't looking forward to it. Without work, she wouldn't have anything to take her mind off Gabe's snub. On top of that, because he'd picked her up at her place, it was no longer a Gabe-free memory zone. But she couldn't put off the inevitable. Sooner or later she had to go home.

Without the protection of the building, when she got closer to her car a cold wind hit her full force. She told herself that's what made her eyes water. Because it couldn't be tears. She was a doctor. And she especially didn't cry over a man.

After pulling out of the parking lot onto Mercy Medical Parkway, she went through the traffic light on Eastern Avenue and kept going until she saw the lights from Green Valley Ranch, her cue to make a right on Paseo Verde. A quarter of a mile up the road, she turned into her complex and touched her remote control to open the guard gates. When they slowly swung wide, she pulled through and turned left. Halfway down the street on the left was her place, and she saw a familiar silver BMW parked at the curb in front.

Her heart stuttered, then started to pound when she saw a familiar man get out of it. "Gabe," she whispered.

She wasn't sure whether or not to be happy, but the adrenaline rush of seeing him pushed away her sadness. She was grateful for that. If the last week had taught her anything, it was to not have expectations. In fact, she hadn't even realized they were there until every one was not met, followed swiftly by a deep hurt. So she was going to assume he had a purpose for being here that had nothing whatsoever to do with her. But she couldn't help wishing she was dressed in something nicer than her powder-blue scrubs and a ratty old sweater.

She parked in the garage, then walked out and met him in the driveway. He had a big, flat cardboard box in his hands that looked suspiciously like pizza. There was a bag on top and a bottle of wine under his arm. "Hi, Gabe."

"Hello, Rebecca."

"What are you doing here?" It was a natural question. On the other hand, her voice sounded unnatural, strained. Defensive? Not if there was a God.

"I wanted an update on Amy. I missed her appointment today."

Rebecca wasn't very good at playing dumb, but she really sucked at hiding her feelings. The thing is, she didn't want him to know she'd missed seeing him because that would make her *look* as stupid as she *felt*. "Really?"

"Yeah. Jack took over for me today."

"Oh. Amy didn't mention it."

Technically that was true. It wasn't until they'd gone to the waiting room that she'd known for sure Gabe wasn't there. But once you started playing dumb, bluffing the rest seemed prudent.

"So, what's the scoop?"

"Gabe, you know the rules."

He lifted the box. "I brought pizza."

She sniffed and her stomach growled. "Pepperoni?"

"Is there any other kind?"

When he grinned, her stomach started acting really weird and it had nothing to do with a hunger for food. She had a bad feeling all the pepperoni in the world wouldn't take the edge off what ailed her.

She put her hands on her hips and pretended indignation. "Do I look like the kind of doctor who can be bought off with a pepperoni pizza?"

He lifted one broad shoulder. "If the stethoscope fits…"

"Okay, then. Come on in." She led the way through the garage and into the house. In the laundry room she slid off her shoes, then reached around and turned on the kitchen lights before glancing over her shoulder. "I don't have much to go with this."

In fact, she had nothing. But she didn't care. She was ridiculously happy to see him.

"I brought salad and wine." He set everything on the kitchen table, then opened her vertical blinds to let in the view of the Las Vegas Strip. "If you have a corkscrew and some glasses, I'll do the honors."

"Coming right up."

Rebecca scrounged through the drawer closest to the table and found the tool, then reached in the cupboard up above and grabbed two wineglasses. "Here you go."

Going, going, gone, she thought, really looking at him. He'd hung his brown leather jacket on the back of a chair and was just rolling up the long sleeves of his casual white shirt. Worn jeans fit his muscular legs like a second skin. The whole look worked for her in a really big way—starting with his thick, wavy, dark-blond hair. The effect continued with his straight white teeth and a smile that should be declared a lethal weapon or a miracle cure. His appeal extended, but was not limited to his broad shoulders and a wide chest that tapered to his flat abdomen and narrow hips. He was a beautiful man. And—best of all—he was *here*.

Her heart was beating so fast she'd blow a pacemaker if she had one. And it was time to get a grip.

She turned away and gathered a couple of placemats, paper plates, napkins and utensils and set the table where he'd poured red wine and opened the salad and pizza boxes.

"Dinner is served," he said, pulling back a chair for her.

"Thank you." She sat and settled herself while he took the seat beside her.

He held up his glass. "What should we drink to?"

"Why do we have to drink to anything?"

"Do you question everything?"

"Inquiring minds want to know," she said, then took a bite of pizza.

He shook his head, blue eyes twinkling. "With that big brain of yours, I bet you were a pain in the ass to your teachers."

"You'd win that bet," she said proudly. "But curiosity is a doctor's best friend. Some conditions are a mystery. Symptoms are clues and we have to figure out what's going on."

"Speaking of that, how's Amy?" He bit into his pizza and chewed while he waited for an answer.

"She's fine. Still not emotionally engaged in what's going on. I tried to tell her that she needs to be ready to care for a baby, but she was unreceptive. Said you would help and can do anything."

His mouth pulled tight for a moment before he said, "She's got that wrong."

"You won't help?"

"No. I'm not superman."

"You don't have to be." He didn't look convinced and she decided to change the subject. "So where is Amy tonight?"

"Jack took her out to dinner."

"I'm sure dinner with a good-looking guy will make Amy feel better." It was working for Rebecca.

"You think Jack is good-looking?"

"Oh, please. Is George Clooney a troll?" she asked. "Of course Jack is handsome. Grace thinks so, too."

"Hmm. What does Grace think about me?" He sent her a warning look. "If the word *troll* pops into your head, I'd appreciate it if you'd consider rephrasing."

"What pops into my head is that you're *trolling* for compliments."

"That was bad, Doc."

"Really? I thought it was quite clever."

"You're too smart for your own good."

He was too sexy for *her* own good, and her nerve endings were buzzing. And the alert level never lowered as they laughed and bantered while finishing dinner. Afterward, Gabe helped her clean up, which amounted to throwing the paper stuff away and putting forks in the dishwasher. By silent agreement they moved over to the corner group in front of her fireplace and set their wineglasses down on the glass coffee table. Rebecca sat and Gabe picked the place right beside her, close enough to smell the scent of his aftershave and feel the heat of his skin.

The adrenaline haze was fading, letting in a healthy dose of reality. Her ridiculously happy phase had passed and she wondered if he'd missed Amy's appointment because he was avoiding her. But if that was the case, why was he here now? Inquiring minds wanted to know.

She angled her body sideways. "So, why did Jack bring Amy into the office today?"

"I was held up by an unscheduled meeting with the hospital's regional president," he explained. "He wanted to discuss phases two and three of the Mercy Medical expansion project. Rule number one in business school says that when establishing yourself in a new market, never give your first client a reason to be less than completely satisfied. You don't often get a second chance to make a first impression."

"So you're not avoiding me?"

The words bypassed her brain-to-mouth filter and were out before she could stop them. More than anything she wanted them back because they just screamed geek alert. It was a subtle reminder, or maybe not so much, that she'd pushed him away. So far he hadn't asked any questions and she would prefer not to answer any.

"I'm not avoiding you." Gabe's eyes darkened even as the corners of his mouth curved up. "Definitely not avoiding you. In fact—"

She slid both legs up on the couch and tucked them beside her as she faced him fully. "What?"

"Well, I was just wondering what you think about kissing."

If *he* was involved, she was all in favor of it. "Kissing is a unique form of communication and involves a large part of the brain."

"Oh?" He looked amused. "That would explain why you're such a good kisser."

"I am?" She was confused.

"On more than one occasion you've told me how smart you are. That must mean you have a very big brain." His nostrils flared slightly, as if he were scenting her and she turned him on.

"I...I can certainly retain a lot of information," she said, her voice slightly breathless. "For instance—did you know that kissing is good for your health?"

"Really?" He was still amused, but the rise and fall of his chest was faster.

"Oh, yes. Let me think." She tapped her lip. "It slows the aging process. Kissing helps tone cheek and jaw muscles so they're less likely to sag."

"That's vanity, not good health."

"Okay. Then how about this? It speeds up metabolism and helps burn calories."

"I'm all in favor of that." He reached out a finger and traced her lips.

Her own respirations escalated by a lot. "It relieves tension. Breathing becomes deeper and eyes close, which is what you do to relax."

"I'm not feeling especially relaxed at the moment."

That made two of them. But he wasn't making a move and

she desperately wanted him to. "I read somewhere that it helps prevent tooth decay."

"Now you're pulling my leg."

She held up her hand, palm out. "Word of honor. It stimulates saliva flow and brings plaque levels down to normal."

His eyes burned into hers. "Right now, I'd have to say all of my levels are anything *but* normal."

Her heart started racing. "It's also a cardiovascular workout. If it's exciting, you release adrenaline into the bloodstream and the heart pumps more blood around your body."

"All around? Or certain parts?" he asked, his voice deep, seductive, his gaze challenging, intense.

Automatically her gaze dropped—*there*—and she swallowed hard. She decided to ignore the question. "And then there are the pheromones."

"Tell me about those."

"They're the chemical messengers that signal sexual attraction."

"I see." He slid closer, so close that his shoulder brushed hers. "Let me see if I understand. Kissing is essentially an exchange of information between two people."

"Yes," she said.

"It's the ultimate chemistry experiment just this side of sex."

"That's one way to look at it," she agreed.

"And science is your thing," he added softly.

"I...I suppose."

"So when are you going to get scientific with me?"

"What are you saying?"

She wasn't stupid. She had a pretty good idea that he was asking if she wanted to have sex. That was kind of a no-brainer. Her hormones hadn't been this happy—well—ever. And he hadn't even touched her yet. Which could be why she was swamped with need. She didn't have a lot of experience.

The first time didn't count. It was violence, not sex. If she could thank her fiancé for anything, it would be for getting her through any postassault physical doubts and fears. But he'd also taught her that losing trust could be as bad as the physical betrayal—when faith was gone you felt just as bad. She didn't want to put herself in a position where she experienced either again.

This was just sex. A basic biological function. They were two people who were mutually attracted—and this was the most important part—consenting adults. To be here like this with Gabe felt so good, especially because she'd thought he was avoiding her.

And this was the biggest problem with her brain. She thought things to death. She was so tired of analyzing everything. For this moment in time she just wanted to *feel.*

"Rebecca?" He trailed his finger beneath her chin and nudged it up. "Do you really not understand what I'm asking?"

"I understand." She met his gaze. "And here's my answer."

Rebecca leaned forward, and no part of her body touched his except where their lips met. Just as she remembered, his mouth was soft, yielding, and he smelled...umm...he smelled like sun and spice and good enough to make her pheromones moan. Before she could censor herself, a soft sound of satisfaction seemed to slide out of her throat, and the next thing she knew, he'd tugged her gently into his lap.

She wrapped her arms around his neck and pressed herself against him. When he cupped her ribs with one big hand and brushed his thumb across the underside of her breast, a punch of pleasure rocked her. They looked at each other for a long moment, then their mouths came together again in a chaos of hunger and heat and heart-pumping passion. She couldn't taste him deeply enough and when he traced her lips with his tongue, she eagerly opened to let him inside. Taking full advantage, he plundered the inside of her mouth with his tongue.

He groaned as he cupped her face in his wide palm and brushed his thumb over her cheek, as gently erotic as when he'd touched her breast.

She let her fingers slide through the hair at his nape and traced the span of his shoulders and the muscles that bunched beneath his shirt. He was so strong and so gentle at the same time. A feeling of tenderness welled up inside her, so big and wide and deep that it was almost painful.

He kissed her cheek, the underside of her jaw, and nibbled her neck, his mouth leaving a trail of tingles wherever he touched.

"Gabe?" Did that husky, needy voice really belong to her?

"Hmm?"

"I...I don't think—" She sucked in a breath and shivered when he kissed an especially sensitive spot just beneath her ear.

"What don't you think?"

"You didn't see the upstairs last time you were here," she pointed out, far too rationally, considering the fact that her body was in danger of going up in flames.

"Is your bedroom up there?" His voice was deep and raspy.

"Yes."

He stood with her in his arms. "Lead the way."

"You have to put me down first."

"Do I have to?" he asked, his lips against hers.

"I'm afraid you'll hurt your back and that would make me sad. Very, very sad."

He smiled as he removed his arm from beneath her legs and let them slide down his front. "I don't want that."

"It's not my first choice, either."

She took his hand and showed him the way up the stairs and through the double doors at the top that led into her bedroom. Light from the hall trickled in. Her queen-size bed was unmade and she'd never been more grateful that she'd been running late that morning. She stopped beside it and he stepped behind her, sliding his arms around her waist as he pulled her against him. She could feel the hard evidence of his desire, and exhilaration rolled through her. He really wanted *her.*

"This is my room."

"Nice room." He nuzzled her throat. "Nice neck."

"I'm glad you like it."

"Rebecca, I— You need to know—"

"What?" she asked, covering his hands with her own.

His breath caressed her cheek. "I haven't done this in a very long time."

"Okay."

"Really. I'm not kidding."

She frowned. "Are you trying to talk me out of it?"

"God, no." His arms tightened around her. "I just don't want you to expect—"

She half turned and kissed his jaw as the devastating tenderness filled her again. "I only expect you to be you."

"I can do that," he said.

Then he moved his hand to the front of her scrub pants and tugged the tie until the waistband loosened. Her heart went from normal sinus rhythm to a cardiovascular workout in the blink of an eye. Her pulse throbbed when he slid his hand inside her panties, slipping a finger between her legs and finding the nub where all the nerve endings of pleasure came together. She gasped and would have crumpled at his feet if he hadn't been holding her.

With a sweeping gesture, he brushed her clothes down and she kicked them off. She pulled the hem of her scrubs top over her head and tossed it aside, then unhooked her bra and let it drop from her fingers. He was still behind her and lifted his hands to cup her breasts. The touch snapped a nearly uncontrollable wanting through her system.

She turned and started to unbutton his shirt, but he saved time and simply pulled it over his head. Then he slid off his shoes, unbuckled his belt and swept off his jeans and boxers and stood before her, completely naked and deliciously male.

Trembling with desire, she ran her hand over the dusting of hair on his wide chest. "You are definitely you."

"And you are so beautiful I—" His eyes darkened with intensity as he shook his head. "I don't have the words to tell you how beautiful you are."

"You don't have to say that. I'm a sure thing."

"It's the God's honest truth."

He swept her into his arms and settled her in the center of the bed. Before joining her, he took something from the pocket of his jeans, then met her gaze and grinned his Gabe grin.

"I…I didn't even think about—" she stammered.

"I did." He shrugged. "I hoped."

After putting on the condom, he stretched out beside her and took her in his arms. He lowered his head and kissed her slow, long and deep. It was a drugging kiss that churned her into a frenzy of need. The wanting couldn't wait, and he must have felt the same, because he parted her thighs then moved between her legs and slowly, gently entered her. She sighed with a relief that was short-lived as he started to move. Slowly at first, then as she caught his rhythm, he stroked deeper and faster taking her higher and higher. Too soon, her body seized around him as her eyes seemed to roll back in her head and indescribable pleasure exploded through her.

Moments later Gabe's face tightened and he went still for seconds before groaning out his own release. Spasms racked his body and his breathing was heavy and fast.

When it was over, he smiled down at her, an achingly sexy and warm expression on his face. "Kissing is relaxing, but sex is the ultimate stress reliever."

"Does being right ever get old?" she asked, utterly and completely relaxed and satisfied.

"It's a gift."

He kissed her softly, then rolled out of bed. Moments later the light in her bathroom went on.

Cold without his presence beside her, Rebecca pulled the sheet up over her nakedness as a scary thought took hold. It hadn't just been sex after all. It wasn't just a simple biological function. For her, sex would never be simple. If she trusted a man enough to be intimate, she was already in a lot of emotional trouble. Because if she risked again, and lost again, she wasn't sure she could recover.

Again.

Chapter Ten

Gabe made love to Rebecca once more when he came back to bed. He'd already crossed the line, a line he shouldn't have, so was there any more harm done?

He told himself the first time hadn't been his finest hour and he felt he owed her. But deep down he knew it was more than that. One taste of her sweet and unexpectedly innocent response when he'd touched her in a certain way, in a certain spot, hadn't been enough for him. Maybe it was because he'd wondered whether or not she would let him touch her at all. After the way she'd reacted the night he'd brought her home, he'd begun to consider the possibility that she'd experienced something bad, something like she said might have happened to Amy. But he didn't understand why she wouldn't tell him.

When she'd been sitting downstairs looking like temptation for the taking all the while touting the benefits of kissing in that sweet, sexy voice, he'd wanted to pull her into his arms and play science until they proved the validity of every single one of those silly suppositions.

Instead, he'd held back and let her take the lead. Man, she'd taken the lead. Led him around like a puppy after a treat. Then she'd treated him again, and the best part was her snuggled in his arms right now, and he tightened his hold. Having a passenger in his car wasn't the only thing he'd missed.

He stroked the smooth, soft skin of her arm. "How are you?"

"Definitely not stressed," she said, brushing her hand over his chest.

The movement rubbed her body against his and stirred him again, partly because it wasn't meant to, and partly because he couldn't get enough of her. To throw a little light on the subject, he reached beside him and turned on the bedside lamp.

Rebecca covered her eyes and pulled the sheet up to cover her body, as if he hadn't just recently seen and kissed almost every inch of her. As if he didn't already know her by heart.

"Bright light," she said.

"I want to see that beautiful face."

Translation: he wanted to see her eyes glaze over when he pleasured her and her full lips part when he relieved her stress.

"You are such a liar," she scoffed.

"Which part? That I want to see you?"

"No. The beautiful part."

He tapped her nose. "That's where you're wrong, brainiac. You're a knockout. I had to warn Jack away. He started drooling when he first saw you in the hospital cafeteria."

"Really?"

"As God is my witness." Gabe stared into her big, guileless eyes and realized she wasn't being coy or fishing for compliments. She genuinely didn't get what a head-turner she was.

What other facets of her personality was she keeping secret? he wondered. He glanced around her room and noticed the lamp was sitting on a box, not yet unpacked. Across from the bed was a dresser with no mirror above it and no pictures or perfume bottles on top. Now that he thought about it, her bathroom hadn't been filled with makeup and hair stuff, either. He hadn't realized he'd expected to see that until he hadn't. Downstairs there weren't any pictures on the white walls or photos casually scattered around. Or even knickknacks.

He knew she hadn't lived there long, but the place was almost barren, devoid of clues about who she was and what her life had been like. No pictures, posters or souvenir ticket stubs from a concert. It was nothing like the home Hannah had made. She couldn't wait to put her personality in the rooms and paint one wall in a bold accent color. He used to tease her about running out of wall space to hang things.

Gabe waited for the knot of pain to tighten in his chest the way it always did when he thought of Hannah. It was disconcerting when the memories only produced a bittersweet warmth instead.

"You're awfully quiet all of a sudden," Rebecca commented.

"Light does that to me."

"How diplomatic. More likely you got a good look at this face and changed your mind."

"Hardly," he said, then kissed the tip of her nose. "I was just wondering about you."

"What does that mean?"

"That I know very little about you."

And he wanted to know everything. Jack was right. He'd been living, but not really *living*. He'd been so wrapped up in his own grief and pain, he hadn't cared to know anything about anything or anyone unless it concerned work. But meeting Rebecca had changed that and he wasn't sure it was a good thing. Not that holding her wasn't good. Really good with an exclamation point. But what about tomorrow?

"There's not all that much to know," she said.

"I disagree. But let's start with what I've got. Your parents are accountants—and technically that's not personal information. You skipped grades in school. You're a doctor. And you're really, really smart. And young. And beautiful."

"You think you can flatter information out of me?" Her eyes were warm with humor.

"Maybe," he said. "I suspect flattery is torture because you don't know how to deal with it."

"Are you playing doctor?"

He grinned. "I'd be happy to play doctor anytime, but right now I'm more interested in knowing you."

"You're not going to take no for an answer, are you?" she asked.

"That's not my plan. Let's start with how you can't take a compliment."

She shrugged. "I'm a brainer geek. And in my defense I'd like to say that they didn't offer classes on learning to gracefully accept compliments in medical school. In fact, there weren't all that many compliments handed out then, or during my internship and residency."

"Now that's what I'm talking about," he said. "Tell me about that time."

"I was busy. So much to learn. Not enough sleep. It was hard."

"More details, please."

"It was *very* hard."

"Not funny, Doc."

"What else do you want to know?"

Good question. He wanted to know what she wanted to tell. Starting with: Was there time for a boyfriend? Had she ever been in love? Did she want to be?

But he couldn't ask that. He had no right when he didn't

want to be. Instead he said, "How did you choose your medical specialty?"

She was quiet for so long he thought she wasn't going to answer. Finally she said, "I think the seed was planted the first time I saw a baby born."

"So you like babies?"

"Not in the 'woman sees baby…woman's biological clock is ticking…woman must have baby' way."

"How, then?"

She sighed. "I thought it was extraordinary. A brand-new life coming safely into the world. Knowing all the factors that make a successful birth. It was, quite simply, the most beautiful thing I'd ever seen. A miracle."

That sort of put into perspective his comment about her being beautiful. Compared to the miracle of birth, she didn't put her looks on the top ten. He found that refreshing, endearing. The way his heart skipped made the revelation downright dangerous.

"So, that's how you decided what you wanted to be when you grew up?"

"That started the ball rolling. And delivering babies is a deeply satisfying aspect of what I do. But I chose this field of medicine because I wanted to work with and help women."

It was her phrasing and the tone that really caught his attention. Women. Not couples or people in general. She'd specifically chosen a specialty that was all about women. And just like that he remembered the panic on her face when she awakened suddenly and pushed him away. When the question wouldn't leave him alone, he had to ask it.

"Did you choose your specialty to avoid men?" Because he was still holding her, he felt her body tense. "What, Rebecca?"

"Nothing."

Was it also nothing that made her suddenly pull out of his arms? She rolled off the bed and disappeared into the shadows beyond the circle of light. When she came back, she'd put on a serviceable pale-yellow terry-cloth robe, belted tightly at the waist.

She looked down and there were definitely shadows in her eyes, although she was standing in the light now. "It's getting late, Gabe," Rebecca said, then left the room.

What just happened? Gabe sat up and dragged his fingers through his hair. One minute she was relaxed and funny. The next she was tossing him out. He'd hit a nerve and that's what he wanted to know about.

He rolled out of bed and got dressed, then went downstairs where she was making a cup of tea. She didn't offer him one and he'd have turned it down, anyway. Nothing short of whiskey neat would have suited his mood.

"What's wrong, Rebecca?"

She didn't look at him for several moments and he suspected she was putting her "doctor" face on. When she turned, her expression gave nothing away. "There's nothing wrong, Gabe. Like I said, it's getting late."

"Not that late." He stood on the other side of the bar and rested his elbows on the granite. "Tell me why you suddenly clammed up."

"I don't know what you mean."

"I *mean* one minute we were basking in the post-coital glow. Bantering, better known as pillow talk, which I was enjoying very much. Then you pulled your head back in your shell because I asked if you do what you do to exclude men from your work."

"I don't exclude men. Every day there are expectant fathers in my office, supporting their wives through a pregnancy that involves their child."

"But technically the man isn't your patient."

"That's true."

He walked around the bar and stood in front of her. "And you're trying to change the subject. Where did you go, Rebecca?"

"I'm right here." She glanced at the clock. "Speaking of going, Amy will wonder where you are."

"If she's worried, she can call my cell."

"Her pregnancy is advanced and she shouldn't be alone, Gabe."

He put his hands on his hips and glared at her. "Are you throwing me out?"

Her gaze raised to his chest and stayed there for several moments while the pulse in her neck beat really fast. Then she looked up, a stubborn set to her delicate jaw. "I'm just saying it's late and I have to work tomorrow. As I'm sure you do."

He knew there was something she wasn't telling him. He also knew nothing he said would change her mind about that and it really ticked him off.

"Have it your way," he said, and headed for the door.

He thought she would follow, but she didn't, and he strongly suspected it had a lot to do with not wanting a good-night kiss as he left. It would be intimate, and he got that. But they'd just been as intimate as a man and woman could be, yet there was a part of herself she wouldn't share. The more closed off she was, the more he wanted to know. That's when he realized he was getting sucked into her.

Gabe knew that was a signal that he'd moved forward in the grieving process. He'd taken a step away from Hannah, a step closer to feeling something—something big—for another woman. He didn't want to feel anything, and Rebecca's attitude should have been a relief.

It was damned annoying when he realized he wasn't relieved at all.

* * *

Rebecca leaned back in her chair and tossed her glasses on her desk. Grace was in the front office filing, billing and answering the phones. Today was the day for patients only in the morning, and the afternoon was to catch up on paperwork. Last night was the night she proved to Gabe beyond a shadow of a doubt that she was too much trouble for him to bother with.

When he'd asked if she was throwing him out, she could only think that he was way too big for that. She desperately had wanted to ask him to stay the night, but she couldn't have done that. Better for him to think she was a whack job than risk another flashback panic attack when she woke with a man beside her. Just one and her fiancé had insisted she tell him about the assault. That's when he'd broken the engagement because she was too needy for him. After the way Gabe had looked at her, Rebecca didn't expect to see him in her bedroom ever again. That was sad; she liked him a lot. And he was a superior kisser. The sex was great, too. The only silver lining she could find was that she'd ended it on her terms.

I am Woman, she thought. Hear me roar.... Whimper was more like it.

She put her glasses on and continued her charting until talking—back-and-forth conversation type talking—from the front office caught her attention. She heard a man's deep voice, then Grace's infectious laugh. Maybe Jack O'Neill had stopped by. The two had seemed to hit it off yesterday when he'd brought Amy in for her appointment.

She stood and stretched, then pulled her office door wide and poked her head out. The man's voice came to her more clearly and it was familiar, except it wasn't Jack's. Her heart beat faster when she recognized Gabe. What was he doing here?

Rebecca figured it must have something to do with Amy

because after last night there's no way he would want to see her except in a professional capacity. Then the conversation stopped and Grace came out of the office and into the hall.

She stopped when she saw Rebecca in the doorway. "Gabe Thorne is here."

"I heard." Rebecca didn't move.

"Aren't you going to talk to him?"

"What does he want?"

"He wants to see you."

"Did he say why?"

Grace slid her a funny look. "I didn't actually ask."

"Isn't part of your job to screen people who come to see me?"

"Only when you're busy with patients. Which you're not today." Grace folded her arms over her chest. "Do you not want to see him? Because I can get rid of him for you."

"No. Yes." She bit her lip. "I don't know."

She wanted to see him. And she didn't. If she spent any more time with him he was going to start asking questions that she didn't want to answer. He was becoming too important, so important she knew it would hurt when he washed his hands of her. The best thing would be to walk away before it got to that point.

"No," she said to Grace.

"What's up with you, Rebecca?"

"It's complicated."

"Okay. Then you can explain it to Gabe yourself."

Grace spun on her heel and walked out before Rebecca could stop her. She went back in her office because running away was wimpy and locking her door childish. Then Gabe stood in her doorway.

"Hi."

"Hi," she said back.

"You're not seeing patients this afternoon."

"How did you know that?" she asked.

"Amy told me."

Rebecca made sure all her patients were aware of office hours and how to reach her when she wasn't in the office.

"Is your sister all right?"

He nodded. "Jack's with her. She's doing some filing for him. Light clerical stuff."

"I think that's really good for her. It will make her feel productive without being too physically strenuous. I hope you're paying her."

"I'm putting it toward her room and board."

"Gabe, she's family—"

He put up his hand. "That was a joke. Of course I'm paying her."

He was a nice man. It would be so much easier if he wasn't.

"If Amy's fine, then I'm not sure why you're here." After last night. But she didn't say that out loud.

"I'm here to break you out of this place."

"I don't understand."

"You have the afternoon off. I have the afternoon off. We're going to do something."

"Why?" What she wanted to say was why would he bother, but her brain-to-mouth filter was actually on for a change.

"Because you work too hard and you need to have some fun."

"Work is fun."

"It won't be if you burn out," he said. "The way to avoid that is regular rest and relaxation."

"Good advice. I appreciate it. And I'll do that as soon as I finish my paperwork." She looked up at him and felt as if her racing heart hit a speed bump. "Thanks for stopping by."

"My pleasure." He folded his arms over the impressive chest that had been even more impressive with his shirt off. "Just so you know, I'm not leaving here without you."

"I'm sorry?"

"I'll sit here or out front in the waiting room until you're ready to go with me."

"I'm not going anywhere with you," she said, just so they were clear. "I have work to do."

"What part of 'I'll wait until you're ready to go' did you not understand?"

This was crazy. "I thought you had inspections and building stuff going on. Why aren't you in your office working?"

"The inspections are done for now. I've been working twenty-four/seven for way too long and I need some time off."

"Very wise, Gabe. Don't let me stand in your way." She rounded her desk and sat down. "Bye."

"Are you throwing me out again?"

Her gaze jumped to his, but the anger and annoyance she'd seen last night were gone. There was only charm and humor in his expression. Why wouldn't he take no for an answer?

"Yes, actually. I am throwing you out. If that's what it takes." She picked up her pen and clicked it open and closed. "Look, Gabe, you and I— I don't think it's—"

"Don't make this complicated, Rebecca. We're two people relatively new to Las Vegas. I hear Red Rock Canyon is pretty spectacular and not to be missed. I'd like company when I go. Have you been there yet?"

"No, but—"

"I didn't think so, what with the workaholic thing you've got going on. So, here's the deal. Do you want to be one of those people who never take the time to see the natural wonders in her own backyard?" He held up a warning finger. "Don't you dare say yes."

His grin was so slow, so sexy and his eyes so smoky, she forgot what she was going to say.

She tried to stop the smile, she really did. But her mouth refused to cooperate with the rational part of her mind warning that she was playing with fire if she gave in.

Without a word she stood up. It was pathetically easy for him to talk her into putting work aside. Maybe that was because she'd always been a nose-to-the-grindstone girl. More likely it had to do with the fact that she just couldn't turn down the chance to be with him.

"You know, Gabe, you're not nearly as cute as you think you are."

"Yes, I am."

Yes, he was. And so much more than just a pretty face. But he'd been to hell and could never come back from that. She couldn't trust him with the secret of her own hell. He was right. She was making this way more complicated than necessary. It was a couple of hours looking at rocks. How romantic could that be? How dangerous?

She knew how things were with him. It's not like she was risking a fall, emotionally speaking.

After following Rebecca home and waiting while she changed clothes, Gabe took the 215 Beltway East and exited at Charleston Boulevard, then followed the signs to the Red Rock Canyon Visitors' Center. He stopped at the entrance and paid the five-dollar-per-car admission price, then drove up the road toward the group of buildings at the top of a slight rise.

After parking, he and Rebecca got out and walked up two sets of stairs and went inside where the Bureau of Land Management operated the gift shop and a series of exhibits depicting wildlife, a history of the area and a display of scenic photos entered in a photographic contest.

Gabe watched Rebecca wander through and stop to read all the information, fascinated by the indigenous animals and plants. He was far more fascinated by the way she filled out a pair of jeans. She bent to look through a microscope at something that caught her attention and he studied her butt, which was pretty amazing. He'd seen her in scrubs, more often than not covered by a white lab coat, and a little black dress that could revolutionize CPR, but until today he'd never seen that her curves were made to wear denim.

She straightened, turned, then her eyebrows rose when she realized he'd been staring. "So, there's quite a bit of stuff here. I had no idea."

That made two of them. "It's pretty interesting."

"I didn't realize that bats were such an important part of ecology."

"Yeah." He glanced up at the printed information on the wall. "They've been maligned for that whole vampire, blood-sucking, neck-biting thing."

Although he knew for a fact how it turned him on to bite her neck. Her hair was pulled on top of her head, revealing the smooth, slender column. If he leaned forward slightly, he could touch his lips to a place that he'd discovered to be very sweet and sensuous. Last night he'd hardly done more than breathe on that very spot to make her shiver and tremble in his arms.

The pulse at the base of her throat beat very fast as she pointed to the words and pictures. "I didn't realize that bats pollinate plants and that entire species are dependant on them for their very existence. Who knew that just to attract the bats these flowers bloomed at night?"

She'd certainly bloomed at night, he thought. She'd opened up in a way he'd never dreamed and attracted him with her sweet, simple and honest responses.

Then something he'd said had changed her mood and, once again, there was nothing simple about her. He'd told himself that was for the best and he should back off, but he couldn't stop thinking about her. He told himself he'd gone to her office today as a friend. To reach out. The truth was he couldn't stay away—kind of like bats to those night-blooming flowers.

They wandered to their right and passed a series of photographs. One was the valley with the red rocks and the perfect arc of a rainbow. Another was a black-and-white shot of a rabbit in the snow.

After that they walked outside and followed a path past the desert tortoise habitat where the renowned Mojave Max resided.

"I don't see him," Rebecca said, searching the enclosure. "He's probably hiding."

Like you, he thought, looking at her delicate profile. Last night she'd stuck her head out of her shell, then pulled back in. Did she sense danger? From him? He thought she knew him better than that. And today was all about getting her to open up, to let her know he wouldn't hurt her.

There was a path of stepping stones, some with words on them, memorial messages with years of birth and death. Brothers, sisters, children, husbands and wives. Rebecca grew quiet, solemn, and he knew she was reading as they walked. One sentiment made him stumble as he read, "Your spirit is gone but the love is forever."

And he couldn't help thinking of Hannah. He would always remember her beautiful soul. But you couldn't hold that close when the night dragged on and threatened to pull you forever into the darkness.

Halfway around the building the path abruptly ended. It was bare dirt and just waiting for more messages to lost loved ones. And he knew he didn't want to ever again be the one left behind to remember what was gone forever.

They walked back to the patio outside the center and with their backs to the low stucco wall, looked at the hills in the distance. With the lowering sun shining directly on them, the red color was even more vivid and dramatic.

Rebecca sighed and shook her head. "Oh, Gabe. Beautiful is pathetically inadequate to describe the view of those mountains. It's breathtaking."

"I know what you mean," he said, sliding his gaze from her face to the craggy peaks and crevices of Red Rock Canyon.

"Looking at those mountains, I—" She stopped and sighed again.

"What?"

"It's so corny."

"Tell me," he urged.

"It just feels like the beauty fills up my soul." She looked sheepish. "Silly, huh?"

"No."

He knew exactly what she meant. But it wasn't the beauty of nature that got to him. When he looked at her, the empty places in his soul didn't echo nearly so loudly. And that was a problem. He didn't want to love again and risk losing it with nothing to hold on to but a memorial tile and meaningless words.

He'd been an idiot to bring Rebecca here. A moron to give in to the need to see her. She was a doctor, a nurturing spirit committed to making people better. The thing was, he was as better as he wanted to get. He'd loved, lost and was finally coming out on the other side of the darkness.

He didn't think he had it in him to go through that again.

Chapter Eleven

"You're awfully quiet over there." The lights of passing freeway cars highlighted Gabe's face when he glanced at her. "So what did you think of Bonnie Springs?"

About six miles from the Red Rock Canyon Visitors' Center, Bonnie Springs was a hole-in-the-wall tourist attraction. Nestled at the base of some pretty spectacular mountains, the place was a mining town with a Wild-West theme. They had mock gunfights every hour on the hour, a mock hanging and dance revue. *Cheesy* was the first word that came to mind, but being with Gabe made cheesy magical.

Rebecca had just had, if not the best day of her life, then it was somewhere in the top five. But she couldn't tell him that because she didn't intend to spend time with him again. At least not outside of being his sister's doctor.

"It was an interesting place," she finally said.

"Define 'interesting.'"

"Well, the restaurant was rundown, but the burger was pretty good."

"Or you were pretty hungry," he pointed out. "All that fresh air. The outing was good for you."

Not in the long run, and that's what she had to look at. She'd already decided not to comment on how today had affected her. Back to Bonnie Springs. "I've never seen breakfast, lunch and dinner menus pasted on old whiskey bottles."

"Also proving my point that you need to get out more," he said, pulling off the 215 at the Pecos Road exit.

"So *you've* seen menus on whiskey bottles?"

"No. But maybe I need to get out more, too."

That implied getting out more together, and she wasn't going there, so she decided to say nothing.

"Don't go quiet on me again," he warned.

"Right back at you."

"What?"

"You got pretty quiet on the memorial path at the Visitors' Center." She shouldn't ask, but it was the main reason she believed getting out more together with him was heartbreak waiting to happen. "Were you thinking about Hannah?"

"Yeah." His mouth pulled tight for a moment. "It was hard not to. Some of those tiles were testament to relationships that lasted years. Hannah and I never got much of a chance to try."

And losing her had taken all the try-again out of him. He turned onto Paseo Verde and they were almost back to her place. She didn't want the day to end, and yet she knew it was time to end things permanently.

"I think—"

"I think you think too much," he interrupted.

She thought so, too, but it's the way she was wired. "What do you want me to say?"

"Let's talk about the petting zoo."

He didn't want to get heavy. Or he didn't want to talk about Hannah. Either or both proved that putting the brakes on this relationship was a good decision. "It smelled. The peacocks roaming free were beautiful."

"Are you aware, Doctor, that the male of the peacock species is the one with the great tail?"

"I'm sure I heard that somewhere." She laughed. In spite of her dark thoughts, the man could still make her laugh. How unfair was that.

He turned right and pulled up to her security gates, then punched in the code to open them. A minute later he stopped the car in her driveway.

"Thanks for everything, Gabe," she said, opening her car door.

"Aren't you going to invite me in for a cup of coffee?"

"I don't think that's a good idea."

He curled his fingers around her upper arm to stop her from getting out. "What's wrong, Rebecca?"

"Nothing." Not yet. But if she didn't stop right now, something could go very wrong. "I think we should call it a night. And—"

"What?"

"I don't think we should see each other outside the parameters of a professional relationship."

"Are you dumping me, Doctor?"

The coach lights from the garage illuminated his face, and she met his gaze. This was when she really hated her lack of a skills set for awkward social situations. "I don't think I'd phrase it quite like that. It implies a dating history, which we don't have."

He dropped his hand. "I don't know how to respond to that."

"No response is required. Good night, Gabe."

She got out of the car and walked to her front door, settling the strap of her purse over her shoulder. Darned if everything didn't waver and get blurry as tears stung her eyes. The soul she'd so recently filled up with the beauty of the canyon suddenly felt drained and empty.

Because she couldn't really see, it was by feel that she located her keys in the bottom of her purse and managed to find the lock. Once inside, she turned the dead bolt, then leaned her back against the door and felt the moisture welling in her eyes spill over and trickle down her cheeks.

This spontaneous sadness, the deep and profound sense of loss, convinced her she'd done the right thing and just in time. Breaking it off made her cry like a baby, and she hadn't known him that long. How much longer before she was in a place where him walking away could do her heart catastrophic damage?

And she had no doubt he would have walked if she'd told him her secret. The man who had wanted to marry her took off because her hang-ups were too much to handle. Even if Gabe could handle it, after what he'd gone through he wouldn't let himself fall in love. Clearly, the two of them were not meant to be.

Suddenly the doorbell rang, startling her heart into a painful pounding. Her purse slid off her shoulder and thudded loudly on the entryway tile. Since the porch light was still on, she could see Gabe when she peeked through the peephole.

He knocked. "Open up, Rebecca. It's not like you can pretend not to be home."

"Go away."

"We need to talk."

To do that she would have to see him, and that was the last thing she wanted. Her nose was running and her eyes were probably red, matching the blotches on her cheeks. "I don't want to see you."

"I don't care what you want."

She rested her forehead against the door. "Why didn't you just leave?"

There was a long silence before he said, "I couldn't. And just so you know, I'm prepared to have this conversation through the door. That means your neighbors will hear every word."

She wished she could say she didn't care, but it would be a lie. It should have been so easy. She was letting him off the hook. He didn't want a deeply personal commitment so why was he pushing this? The only answers she'd get would be all over the neighborhood if she didn't open the door.

So she did, then stood back to allow him inside.

"Thank you."

"You're not welcome." She sniffled and turned away, then walked into the family room to flip on a light switch.

"Are you crying?" he asked.

"No."

He moved behind her and gently curled his hands around her upper arms. "It's allergies, right?"

"Must be." She sniffled again.

"Rebecca— Don't cry." He turned her and folded her in his arms.

She wanted to push away and she really tried, but she couldn't. "This isn't crying. I'm a doctor. I don't cry."

"That's a lie. And just so you know, I'm glad my sister's doctor cares enough to cry."

The solid feel of his chest beneath her cheek felt too good for words. And she didn't even want to think about what that big warm hand rubbing up and down her back was doing to her. It was turning her spineless, that's what it was doing.

"Please go away."

"Give me one good reason."

"Because you were right. I'm dumping you."

The man had the audacity to laugh. She felt the rumble in his chest even before she heard the full, rich sound of it.

He rubbed his chin on the top of her head. "Let me get this straight. Overall we had fun today, but you don't want to do it again. Is that about right?"

It was so much more complicated, but essentially that was the bottom line. "Yes."

"Why?"

She was a social geek, but not so dense that she didn't realize giving him this information while snuggled in his arms sort of took the power out of her words. "I don't want to see you anymore because this whole thing is not really working for me."

"Define 'this whole thing.'" He put her away from him, just far enough to study her face, look into her eyes.

"You. Me. This—whatever it is—between us. For me, it's just not working."

He cupped her face in his hands and applied the gentle pressure of his lips to hers. Just like that, her female parts were working far too well. Her brain? Not so much, because the next thing she knew they were upstairs in her room beside her bed and she'd started undoing the buttons on his shirt. His hands were busy with the button and zipper on her jeans. They were both breathing heavily.

She pulled back, her chest rising and falling fast, her heart pounding almost painfully. Her voice was raspy when she asked, "Did you not leave because you wanted sex?"

"No." He looked at her, his eyes dark and brooding, intense and blazing all at the same time. "I wanted to leave and I actually drove to the gates before turning around. I couldn't go. I only wanted to talk." He kissed her softly, then smiled. "But I wouldn't turn down sex."

"Okay. Good," she said breathlessly. "Because I think conversation is highly overrated."

"It is at the moment," he said, reaching behind her to unhook her bra, then slide the straps off her shoulders. He cupped her bare breasts in his hands and stared into her eyes as his thumbs did things to her nipples that had definite therapeutic benefits. "I prefer to communicate by touch."

A shaft of heat and need shot straight to that place between her legs, and she moaned softly. "Have I ever told you how incredibly eloquent you are?"

He stared at her face, and an achingly tender expression crept into his eyes. "One look at you is worth a thousand words."

How amazingly sweet was that? And he had her. Right then and there, he had her. She was in for a penny, in for a pound, testing the depth of the water with both feet. Out of the Frying Pan, into the Fire, and every other cliché in the whole world of smart women making unwise choices. But she couldn't find the will to care.

She slid off her shoes, then jeans and panties with one sweeping movement and stood in front of him naked as the day she was born. He did the same. Just looking at him made her want to touch him everywhere. His broad shoulders, muscular arms, flat belly. More than her next breath, she wanted to feel her skin next to his and took a step forward to wrap her arms around his waist and press her breasts to his chest.

His shuddering sigh came from somewhere deep inside, just this side of a groan. "Rebecca— I— You— You feel really good."

She stepped back and looked into his eyes, then lifted his hand to her breast. "I heard somewhere that touch is a superior form of communication."

He swung her easily into his arms, set one knee on the bed before lowering her to the center of the mattress. "Then I intend to have a very, very long conversation with you in a reclining position."

She slid her arms around his neck and smiled. "Okay. Talk trashy to me."

"It's like you can read my mind." He grinned, then brought his lips to hers in a sizzling kiss.

If Rebecca wasn't already flat on her back, she would have been a puddle at his feet. The man could *kiss*. He nibbled her lips, then swept his tongue across the bottom one until she parted for him. He slid inside and skimmed it across the roof of her mouth. Her stomach trembled as he moved his hand from her breast, over her abdomen and teased her legs wider.

Like last time she wanted to go tense, go rigid, but she knew Gabe wouldn't hurt her. And she wanted this. She wanted him. When he moved his hand to that most feminine place between her legs, she gave him full access to the warmth. He slid two fingers inside her, and the touch sent an intense ache down the center of her body, all the way to her toes.

She heard small whimpering cries, and her pleasure-drenched mind took several moments to realize that the sounds came from her. Her back arched and her hips began to rock, starting a rhythm, a willful invitation as the heat balled in her belly.

With his thumb, he touched the small nub that was the center point of her pleasure. When she gasped, he settled his mouth on hers, swallowing her cry of desire. Then he trailed kisses over her cheek, down her throat, flicked his tongue over a spot just beneath her ear and nearly sent her over the edge.

She half turned onto her side, reaching, touching, using her body to communicate her need. When it wasn't enough, she said, "Please, Gabe—" her voice a ragged whisper "I want you. Now—"

"Open your eyes, Rebecca."

"What?"

"Look at me."

She did as he asked, and saw the intensity on his face along with a deep tenderness. "Gabe—"

"Say it again," he rasped. "Say my name,"

"Gabe—"

And she felt the shadows disappear. This was Gabe and she felt safe with him. She trusted him completely.

He nudged her onto her back, then settled himself between her thighs and slowly, gently slid into her waiting warmth. He brushed the hair off her face and kissed her tenderly. She wrapped her legs around him and lifted her hips, taking him more deeply inside. She met him thrust for thrust as he slid slowly, smoothly into her over and over again. His breathing grew faster and faster and her own matched it until her mind went brilliant and her body stilled as sensation after amazingly pleasurable sensation ripped through her. A heartbeat later, Gabe stilled above her as he groaned out his own release.

Rebecca felt all her tension drain away, leaving her limp and satisfied. Intensely relaxed, she curled into Gabe and fell deeply asleep.

Rebecca was dimly aware of someone next to her. Someone strong holding her, on top of her. Fear clawed through her. Her heart pounded. She couldn't breathe. It was happening again. He held her down and jammed his knee between her legs forcing them apart. He was pushing inside of her, hurting her.

"No," she screamed.

She said it over and over but he wouldn't stop.

Panic knotted inside her and she pushed as hard as she could. She heard someone screaming and hands, strong hands grabbed her wrists and held them. Then a man's voice, soothing, calm.

"Rebecca, it's Gabe. Relax, honey. It's okay. Just a bad dream. You're all right…"

She opened her eyes and saw it wasn't that other man. Gabe hovered over her looking worried. And confused. Before she could identify pity, she dropped her gaze to his chest and noticed the deep, angry looking scratches. Had she done that?

She drew in a shuddering breath. "Let me go."

Instantly he released her hands. "Are you okay?"

Not really. But that was more complicated. "I'm awake," she answered.

He stared at her. "What's going on, Rebecca?"

"I have nightmares sometimes." Never hurt to try a bluff.

"Sometimes? With me you're two for two. That changes sometimes to recurring. Talk to me."

She should have known he wouldn't be put off. If he was that easy he would have left when she'd dumped him. The man didn't take no for an answer. How she wished he had.

The reality was that she was the one who'd messed up. She'd been a fool. It had been stupid to pretend that she wasn't in too deep emotionally. Otherwise she wouldn't have slept with him even once, let alone twice. He would be an idiot not to know there was something she was keeping from him. If she blew him off, he was out of there. If she told him her secret, he was out of there. Since either way he would walk, she had no choice. She couldn't help wondering if it would have hurt any less if he'd gone when she'd sent him.

"I'd like to put clothes on," she said quietly.

He nodded and rolled away so she could get up. She slipped into fleece pants and a thick sweatshirt while he dressed. Then they went downstairs and she put on the teakettle.

Gabe sat on one of the bar stools and solemnly watched. Waiting, impatiently she suspected, for her to talk to him. She busied herself with cups and teabags, anything to not have to look at him. She hated that the guy who'd hurt her was still hurting her. She'd hoped she could hide the past, keep it buried.

Then she remembered the night she and Gabe had gone to the benefit. Trish Kendrick had said it was wrong to keep rape a secret. If that was true, she was about to right that wrong.

She turned to look at Gabe. Along with the impatience, she saw a tenderness in his eyes. She should have confided in him that night she'd freaked out. Not keeping the secret didn't mean she had to rent a billboard on Las Vegas Boulevard that said Rebecca Hamilton was sexually assaulted. But when she met someone, at the appropriate time, she needed to talk about what happened to her. Then let the chips fall where they may. She realized that now.

She poured hot water into both mugs, then walked over to Gabe, setting one on the counter in front of him and wrapped her hands around her own steaming cup.

"Are you finished procrastinating?" he asked.

"Just about." She dunked her teabag a couple times. "Okay. I'm ready now."

"Shoot."

She blew out a long breath. "The thing is, Gabe, I have issues."

One corner of his mouth quirked. "You have no idea how badly I want to say 'duh.'"

"I'm so glad you're holding back." Her stomach was jumping and not in a good way. "I was engaged a little over a year ago."

Any hint of a smile disappeared. "I see."

She knew the words were conversational, meant to encourage further communication. But it didn't help the knots inside her. For some reason it was easier to start here than at the beginning. "We didn't get married."

"I gathered that. What happened?"

"He broke it off. Dumped me."

He frowned. "Clearly you're better off."

"You think?"

"Yeah, I think. The man is an idiot."

"I'm not so sure he wasn't justified."

"No way."

"How can you say that?"

"Because the man who's lucky enough to be with you wouldn't be stupid enough to walk away."

She'd felt like damaged goods for so long the words were balm to a battered soul. She let the soothing effects soak in for a moment. Maybe it would give her the courage she needed to tell the rest.

Before she did, she had to ask, "Why would a man be stupid to walk away?"

"Because he gets to be with you."

Again her spirit soared and filled with a hope that shone as bright and beautiful as the sun on the red rocks in the canyon. She tried to smile. "I'm not so sure."

"Did he cheat on you?" The frown turned to a glare. "I'd be happy to beat the crap out of him if you want."

"It wasn't another woman. But I might take you up on your offer." Here's where she had to tell him why. "Our relationship went south after I told him about my past. Some—" She swallowed and gripped her mug until her knuckles turned white. "Something happened and it was a problem for him."

"When you love someone, it shouldn't matter. So the offer of beating him up is still on the table."

"As a doctor I've sworn to do no harm."

"I can see how that would be inconvenient at times."

"No kidding."

"Tell me what happened," he urged.

"I want to. I think it's time. Way past time. *Need* to talk about it would be more accurate." She stared at him without saying anything. After what happened the last time she told someone, it was hard to get the words out.

"Rebecca, I'm here for you. You can tell me. It's like a Band-Aid."

"Excuse me?"

"It's not so bad if you just do it fast. Trust me—"

His phone rang. There was no tune of a song that gave a clue to his personality, or his taste in music. Just a no-nonsense, harsh ring that got Gabe's attention and startled her. He plucked the cell from the holster on his belt.

"Gabe Thorne—" He listened for a moment. "Calm down, Jack. What's wrong?"

Rebecca's stomach dropped. Then she reminded herself the problem could be related to his work, not hers.

"Amy's what?" He ran his fingers through his hair. "What do you mean she's out of it?"

"Let me talk to him," Rebecca said. When he handed her the phone she said, "Jack, this is Rebecca. What's going on with Amy?"

"Rebecca, thank God—"

"Tell me about Amy."

"She said she felt funny. That she didn't feel right. Then she just spaced out."

"Is she conscious?"

"No. What should I do?"

"Call 911. When the paramedics get there they'll start an IV. Tell them to transport to Mercy Medical stat. She's a direct admit to Labor and Delivery. I'll meet her there. Got that?"

"Yeah." He hung up.

Gabe looked at her. "What's wrong with my sister? Is she conscious?"

"Jack said no. I won't know anything for sure until I see her. I have to go."

"I'll drive."

She would have expected nothing less. No matter how badly he might want to, Gabe didn't run out on someone he loved. She didn't have time right now to dwell on the unfairness of it all.

Chapter Twelve

Gabe still hated hospitals. More than ever.

He stood by the window on the second floor and looked out over the lights of the Vegas Valley. He could see The Strip from here, yet it seemed a thousand miles away, pretty far removed from Mercy Medical Center. He could pick out the distinctive green outline of the MGM Grand, the silhouette of New York, New York, and the elegance of Caesar's Palace. But no matter how glitzy and glamorous the view from this window, hospitals still scared the hell out of him.

There was no one else in the waiting room. Somewhere past the double doors Rebecca was evaluating his sister's medical condition. He'd seen the doc shy, embarrassed, teasing and in the throes of passion. But he'd never seen her worried the way she was while they'd waited for the paramedics to bring Amy in. She'd gone into action mode as soon as the gurney came off the elevator and Gabe had caught a glimpse of his sister's pale face. She hadn't looked back at him because she was still unconscious. Fear knotted in his belly.

Jack exited the elevator with two steaming cups of coffee and handed one to him. "Any news?"

"Not yet." He looked at his friend.

"It was just dumb luck that I was with her," Jack said. "After work I was giving her a ride home, like you asked. I hate eating alone and in spite of what you think it happens a lot. Amy and I got a bite to eat. She looked as if she was enjoying being out and I suggested a movie. When I dropped her off at the house, she said she was feeling weird, so I went in with her." He shrugged. "You know the rest."

"I should have been there," Gabe said.

Jack stared at him. "Because you know so much more about emergency situations that you could have handled it better than me?"

"Of course not. You did fine." He ran his fingers through his hair. "But she's my sister. I just should have supported her better, that's all."

"You are supporting her, Gabe. You gave her a place to live and a job. You're helping her get on her feet. You're here. You look like you want to punch something. Or someone. But you're here. How much more could you have done if you'd been there?"

"I don't know. Made her eat right."

"So now you're the food police?"

"Maybe. I could have spent more time with her. I should have—"

"What? Used Amy for another excuse to put your life on hold?"

"Stick to construction and leave psychoanalysis to the—"

"Psychos?" Jack asked.

He smiled through his anger. Jack had a way of making him

do that. But if he was protecting himself from life, that was his own business. "She's my sister. Brothers are supposed to take care of their sisters."

Jack's face took on a dark, brooding aspect. "And when brothers can't be there, best friends step in. Like you did with Hannah."

"I loved her," Gabe said simply. It didn't escape his notice that he'd used the past tense. And this wasn't the time to figure out why or how he felt about that.

"I know you did." Jack nodded. "And I love Amy. She's the closest thing I have to a little sister."

The other man held his hands out in a helpless gesture. "Gabe, she scared the crap out of me. I didn't know what to do."

"You did everything right." If only he could say the same for himself, Gabe thought. Instead of taking care of his sister, he'd been out having a good time.

Seeing Rebecca, spending time with her had seemed so important. She smoothed out his painful edges. She made him feel better with a single smile. To watch her eyes glow with teasing humor was like a drug, and every time he was with her he needed more. Was it so wrong to want to keep the darkness at bay and bask in her light?

At least because they'd been together, Rebecca had taken charge and expedited the situation by coordinating the transport and alerting the staff that she was meeting a patient here. They'd been here waiting when Amy arrived. Now he was still waiting, and he hated how much he wished he was with Rebecca instead of Jack.

Gabe took a sip of hot coffee and it burned his mouth. "Have I mentioned how grateful I am that you were with Amy?"

"Have I ever mentioned how grateful I am that you were with my sister when—" He stopped and let out a breath. "Amy and the baby are going to be fine."

Gabe didn't say anything. He couldn't. His track record on good luck was pretty dismal. But what else was Jack supposed to say?

"So what's with you and the doc?"

He was supposed to say anything but that. Gabe shot him a look instead of answering.

Jack shrugged. "Give me a break. I'm being a friend, trying to take your mind off things."

"You're prying into my personal life."

"So what's your point?"

Gabe shook his head as he blew out a breath. "Heck if I know."

"So tell me what's going on."

Good question. There were those who would say it was a good thing he'd met someone he liked. They would be wrong. It was the worst possible scenario. As far as Gabe could tell, he was doing his damnedest to tread water. He was trying to stay afloat and not let the unwelcome feelings for Rebecca pull him in, pull him under. He never wanted to—

Before he could finish that thought, the double doors opened and Rebecca walked out. He wasn't proud of the fact that he noticed how good she looked in those shapeless green scrubs. And he didn't like how glad he was to see her. More than that, he didn't like the worried look on her face.

She stopped in front of them and smiled at Jack, then met his gaze. "Hi—

"How's Amy?" Gabe demanded.

"Not good."

He could see her weighing her words. "What's going on?"

"She has a condition called eclampsia."

"What's that?"

"It's a severe form of pregnancy-induced hypertension. We gave her magnesium sulfate, IV, to control it—"

He held up his hands. "Stop with the medical jargon and say it in terms I can understand."

"Amy has high blood pressure, and it caused her to have a seizure. The medicine is to help control it."

Gabe couldn't even wrap his mind around that. It sounded bad and all he wanted to know was how to fix it. "What do we do?"

"I need to deliver her baby now. It's a little early, but if we don't the risks to her and the infant are too high. The only treatment is to end the pregnancy. I need to do an emergency C-section."

"But, Rebecca, you've said sometimes it's best to watch and wait. What if—"

Warmth spread through him and stemmed the tide of fear when she put her hand on his arm. "Gabe, there's absolutely no question in my mind that this is the right thing. If I don't do this now, we could lose her, the baby or both of them."

Was this what had happened to his mother? He'd never asked. His father had never discussed it. Gabe only knew his mother went to the hospital to have a baby and he'd never seen her alive again.

"Can I see Amy?"

"She's still unconscious."

"Just for a minute."

Rebecca hesitated and must have seen something in his face, because she nodded. "Okay. But I really need to get her to the O.R."

She turned abruptly, and Gabe followed her through the doors and down the hall. She took him into an exam room where Amy was still on the gurney with an IV in her arm and surrounded by equipment. A white cotton blanket covered the mound of her belly. She looked pale and impossibly young. And so still his chest went tight.

He moved beside her and took her hand. "Hi, kiddo. It's

Gabe. I don't know if you can hear me or not, but I hope you know somehow that I'm here."

"We have to take her up, Gabe."

He glanced over his shoulder. A man and woman in scrubs waited beside Rebecca. She had her doctor face on, and he had no idea what she was thinking. Now that he was here, he didn't know what to say to his sister. What would he have told his mother if he'd had the chance?

He squeezed his sister's hand and brushed the hair back from her face. Then he kissed her forehead. "I love you, Amy."

"Gabe—"

He looked at Rebecca and nodded, then stepped back and let the professionals do their work. They wheeled his sister out of the room and he was left alone with Rebecca.

"Take care of her," he said.

"I will." She met his gaze. "Gabe, you should think about calling your father."

"What are you saying?" he demanded.

"Not that." She held up her hand. "But this is very serious. Amy is his daughter and he should know what's going on with her."

He had nothing to lose now because Amy couldn't run. More important, Rebecca was right.

"I'll let my dad know right away."

"Good." She started for the door.

"Wait—"

"What?" she asked softly.

"Here's the thing, Rebecca. I feel like I just found Amy. Or maybe she found me. I don't know. The point is that we haven't had enough time. I don't want to lose her."

"I'll do my best."

And her best was good because she was really smart. He'd never had more reason to be grateful for that than he was right now. After losing so much, he didn't think he could stand to lose one more person he cared about.

Thank God the C-section had gone well, Rebecca thought. It had only been several hours since she'd delivered the baby, but Amy's condition had stabilized quickly. Rebecca had gone home for a few hours and was back now, on her way to check on the teen. At the end of the hall, she noticed an older man standing outside the newborn nursery. There was something vaguely familiar about the tilt of his head, the strong stubborn chin, the tall, lean body. His khaki slacks and navy knit shirt suggested he'd just left the golf course, but not if he was who she suspected.

She stopped beside him and noticed gray at his temples. But the dark-blond hair was the same shade as his son's. "Mr. Thorne?"

"Yes." He turned away from the window and met her gaze. "And you are?"

"Dr. Rebecca Hamilton." She held out her hand and he shook it.

"Carleton Thorne." After staring for several moments, he said, "You look too young to be a doctor."

"I get that a lot." She smiled, remembering the first time she'd seen Gabe and Amy. It was a day that had changed her life. While she cared about all the women in her care, Amy Thorne had a special place in her heart. So did Gabe.

That's why she was back here at the hospital. She needed to check on her newest mother. She'd talked to the nurses who said the teen was doing very well. Physically. But she was refusing to have anything to do with the baby. For that reason, Rebecca was happy to see this man.

"You got here fast, Mr. Thorne."

"Gabe sent the company Gulfstream and picked me up at

McCarran's Executive Terminal a little while ago." His eyes were blue. Like his son's.

"One's own jet would certainly speed things up," she said, nodding.

It was the middle of the night, but as the prime contractor on the hospital expansion project, Gabe had a badge with the metallic strip that would let him in and out of Mercy Medical at all hours.

"Where is he?"

"Sitting with Amy." His polite expression changed to concern. "How is my daughter? And my grandson?" he said, glancing at the swaddled baby in the isolette on the other side of the window. Because most new mothers wanted their newborns with them, he was one of only a few babies in the nursery.

"Your grandson is approximately four to five weeks early." That was her best guess and only Amy knew for sure if it was right. "He's just over four and a half pounds, a little small, but—" Not as small as she'd feared. Low-birth-weight babies were a problem with teenage mothers who didn't take care of themselves..

"But?"

"He's been checked out by a neonatal intensifist…specialist," she clarified. "We'll watch him carefully, but there's no indication that he won't do well."

"I see." He folded his arms over his chest. "And Amy? Gabe filled me in on the medical factors and the need for an emergency C-section."

"The initial danger is past, but she's not out of the woods for at least forty-eight hours. Hypertension can cause restricted blood flow and tends to affect the brain, liver and kidneys. We're monitoring her for any sign that they're shutting down. It's just a precaution. I'm cautiously optimistic that she'll make a full recovery."

"Thank you, doctor."

"You're welcome."

He stared down the hall, pensive and brooding. Obviously, he'd wasted no time getting to his daughter after Gabe called, and yet he looked lost. Torn between the new life his daughter had brought into the world and the daughter who hadn't wanted him to know she was in trouble.

Rebecca wasn't sure what she expected from him, but anger at being left out of the loop would be at the top of her list. And she saw no evidence of that. He'd lost his wife in childbirth. The motherless child she'd left behind had nearly lost her life. But this was the same child he'd been too heartbroken to notice. She couldn't help being angry about that and did her best not to let it show.

And she had a question outside the parameters of her professional medical obligation. She should walk away. But from the moment she met Amy, and Gabe for that matter, she hadn't been able to walk away when she should have.

"Mr. Thorne, have you seen Amy yet?"

"No." Sadness brimmed in his eyes. But there was something else, too. "I can't imagine what you think of me, Dr. Hamilton. My own daughter threatened to run away if her brother involved me."

"Mr. Thorne—"

"Call me Carleton."

She nodded. "Obviously, you care about Amy or you wouldn't be here now."

"Of course I care. But I'm ashamed to admit I have no idea what's going on with my daughter. I didn't even know she was dating, let alone that she was going to have a baby."

"Were you worried about her when she took off?"

"Of course I was. It was a relief when she called to let me know she was all right. She told me she was with a friend."

Partly true, Rebecca thought. At least, she and Gabe had put down a foundation for friendship. Anger didn't blind her to the reality. "Carleton, you couldn't know what she didn't choose to tell you."

His glance slid to the baby behind the glass. "Our problems go back to when her mother died. My wife was the glue that held the family together. When she was gone, I didn't know what to do, especially with a baby girl."

"You were in shock."

The expression in his eyes was bleak, with overtones of anger. "Apparently it's a condition that's lasted for eighteen years. There is no way to mitigate my culpability, Rebecca. May I call you that?"

"Of course."

"I've let my daughter down and there's no way to fix that."

She put her hand on his arm. "You didn't deliberately disappoint your daughter. It must have been a devastating loss. Amy's mother was a lucky woman to have been loved so deeply." She drew in a breath. "And you're right about one thing. You can't fix the past with your daughter. But the future is up for grabs. You don't have to let Amy down now."

"She doesn't want me to be a part of her life."

"Your daughter doesn't really know what she wants. But I'll tell you this. What she *needs* is support. Someone strong to lean on. I'm concerned about her emotional well-being."

"In what way?"

"She's resisting bonding with her baby. I don't know if the cause is rooted in her childhood and losing her own mother before she ever knew her. Or…something else. Whatever it is, she needs her father more than ever. And if you walk out on her I will personally—"

"Kick his ass?" The familiar voice held a trace of amusement. "Watch out, Dad. She's one tough lady."

Rebecca glanced over her shoulder to see Gabe behind them. He was still wearing the jeans and shirt from yesterday in Red Rock Canyon. It seemed a lifetime ago. Now he was rumpled in the sexiest possible way. And he was solidly there for the people he loved.

"And how do you know this, son?" There was a gleam in the elder Thorne's eyes.

Come to think of it, there was a gleam in the younger Thorne's eyes, too. But Rebecca suspected it was generated by something completely different, something that made her stomach jump and her heart race.

Gabe stood beside her and looked down. "I know because she's really smart. I'd listen to her if I were you."

"I'll do my best."

She nodded. "Let's go see your daughter."

The three of them walked in the room. Rebecca took the lead and saw that Amy was awake. She had an IV going with a small, hand-held pump that allowed her to control her own pain medication.

"There's more color in your face," she said. "Are you comfortable?"

"Pretty much." The teen tensed when she saw her father.

"Hello, Amy."

She didn't say anything and looked more like a sad little girl than the defiant teen Rebecca had first met.

Carleton stood at the foot of the bed. "How are you?"

"Okay."

"I've seen the baby. He's quite something." He cleared his throat. "What are you going to call him?"

"I haven't thought about it."

"My father's name was Matthew."

"So?" The shield of hostility was in place, although it was fuzzy around the edges. Drugs took the edge off the glare she aimed at her father. "Aren't you going to ask how I could be so stupid?"

Rebecca held her breath as she looked between the two. She had her suspicions, but no one knew for sure how this baby had been conceived. The teen had thrown down the challenge, almost given her father a script of how this first meeting was going to go. It was as if she was giving him enough rope to hang himself. He'd never been there for her. She didn't expect him to be there and she was going to give him a reason not to be there now.

Rebecca recognized it in the teen because the behavior was so familiar to her. It was a pattern she knew well.

"That's a loaded question," Carleton told his daughter. "Both a yes and no response imply that I think you're stupid. That isn't the case. You're very bright."

"How would you know? You never paid any attention."

"That's true. And I worked hard at it, too." He met her gaze. "In spite of my shortcomings as a father, some information sank in."

"What's your point?"

"I want to pay attention now."

Amy blinked. "Why? I don't need you now."

"You're wrong." He moved beside her and started to take her hand. He hesitated a moment, then took her fingers in his palm. The body language was stiff, awkward, but it was a start. "I think you need me now more than ever. However, I'm not going to argue. That would be a waste of time and I've wasted enough already. Besides, words are cheap. All I can do is be there for you every day from now on. I need you in my life."

"Since when?"

"Since I thought I was going to lose you," he said, his voice cracking.

"Why should I believe you?"

"No reason on earth. But I'm not going anywhere. You'll just have to get used to it."

Amy looked at her father and for once didn't have a comeback, but the sheen of tears in her eyes spoke volumes. It was a vulnerability Rebecca had never seen in the girl. And it was time for her to leave this family alone and let the healing begin.

She slipped into the hall and leaned back against the wall with a deep sigh. Carleton Thorne was far from perfect, but he was *there*. He'd admitted his fault and he was trying. No one could ask more than that.

She couldn't help thinking how she would feel if she were in Amy's situation. She'd want someone to hold her. In that instant she realized there was nowhere she'd rather be than in Gabe's arms.

She was in love with him.

The realization shouldn't have come as a surprise. Her feelings for him should have been obvious when she'd decided to tell him what happened to her. Instead of joy, she was filled with a deep sadness, because she understood that a positive outcome was hopeless.

Just a few minutes with Gabe's father gave her a pretty good indication that the Thorne men loved with their whole heart and soul. They were one-woman men. And Gabe had already found that one woman. Then he'd lost her. Rebecca didn't have a chance.

Chapter Thirteen

Gabe nodded with satisfaction as he took a last look at the newly installed wallboard of what would be the expanded women's wing of Mercy Medical Center. It was coming along well. And so was his sister. The forty-eight-hour mark had passed and she'd been declared officially out of the woods, which was a major relief. The positive outcome to her medical crisis had gone a long way toward improving his attitude about hospitals. Or maybe it was Rebecca's positive influence. Not only that, one look at her beautiful face had a way of making him see the brighter side of life.

He walked down the construction stairs and left his hard hat with one of the workmen. Since he was already here, he'd drop in and see his sister. He took the elevator down and got off at her floor, then headed toward her room. Their father was making plans to take his daughter home, which also should have been a major relief because that meant his own life would get back to normal.

Then he saw Rebecca walking down the hall and something intense flared through him. His body went hot and tight; his heart jolted. Right then and there he became acutely aware that nothing would ever be normal again after knowing her. That did not make him happy.

He moved toward her and waited expectantly for the sunny smile, but it never came. Apparently she wasn't happy, either, but she was definitely deep in thought—preoccupied and worried. She would have gone right past him if he hadn't reached out and touched her. It was weird, but he knew with absolute certainty that he could never not be absolutely aware of her.

When she didn't respond right away he said, "Rebecca?"

"Hmm?" She looked at him and it took a second or two for her to focus. "Oh. Hi."

"Is something wrong with Amy?"

"No." She hesitated, then said, "Not physically."

"What does that mean?" When she hesitated to answer, he said, "I can see you're concerned. I'd like to know why."

She rested her hands on her hips for a moment, then met his gaze. "Her body is healing and all her tests are normal. From a medical perspective she's doing extremely well."

"But?" he prompted.

"Emotionally we're still at square one."

"Because?"

"She still hasn't seen or held her baby."

The words sliced through him and he thought it just might be a Thorne family failing. He hadn't seen or held his nephew, either. He just couldn't bring himself to do it and face the painful reminder of his own tiny daughter and the smiles he would never see, the milestones the two of them would never share. She'd never talk or take her first steps and he'd never have the chance to walk her down the aisle at her wedding. Not a day went by that he didn't think of her or wonder what she'd look like now.

"She has the option of giving up the child and she's receiving counseling, but… Gabe?"

He must have zoned out because Rebecca was giving him a funny look. Pulling it together he said, "Amy's been through a lot. Give her time."

He took Rebecca's arm and moved her against the wall when two hospital attendants wheeled a bed down the hall toward the elevator.

When she met his gaze, questions swirled in her eyes. "I know you think I'm barely old enough to have a medical license, but I've delivered a lot of babies. I've seen women go through long labors and a great deal of pain associated with giving birth. But all they can think about is holding their baby for the first time. Even when they're planning to give up the baby, usually nothing keeps them from their child—unless there's something wrong."

"You think there's something wrong with Amy?"

"I'm sure of it, and you have to help me get her to talk about what's bothering her."

Gabe glanced away as men and women in scrubs and lab coats passed by. Some had paperwork in their hands, others had stethoscopes draped around their necks. The staff at Mercy Medical was dedicated to healing mind, body and spirit. Rebecca was taking that philosophy very seriously.

Gabe didn't want to go there. "You're always preaching Do No Harm. If Amy doesn't want to talk, there's probably a good reason. Wouldn't it be better to leave well enough alone?"

Her eyes narrowed, sharp and assessing. "A doctor's job is to watch, wait and decide whether a situation will get better on its own or intervention is required. When Amy's blood pressure shot up I took invasive action, absolutely certain it was the right thing to do. I'm equally as certain that her spirit requires invasive action, too."

"Doesn't the hospital have staff for that sort of thing?"

"Of course. As I said, the counselor has been in to see her, but she's not cooperating."

"You know I support my sister. I love her," he said simply. "But maybe she's not ready—"

"There's not a lot of time to wait for her to *be* ready. She'll be well enough to be discharged soon, and she has a baby depending on her. I can't in good conscience send her home with that child to care for—not in her current state." She took a breath and said, "With or without your cooperation I'm going to talk to her and try to get her to open up."

She turned around and walked back to Amy's room. He watched her, the determination in her stride, the sway of her hips, the way she tossed her blond hair back as if it were an annoyance and not the lush and beautiful silk that turned him on and made him ache with need when he'd run his fingers through it.

Gabe watched, fully intending to let her go on this quest alone. He'd made it a point not to see the baby. He certainly didn't want to talk about him. Rebecca could handle this better by herself. But he remembered when Amy had first shown up and how Rebecca had dragged him into the situation against his will. He'd established a relationship with his sister and he was glad about that.

He moved then. Only because he loved Amy, he told himself. As soon as the thought formed he knew it was more than that. It was about Rebecca. He didn't want it to be and was trying to convince himself family loyalty was responsible. That was partly true, but mostly it was for Rebecca.

He followed her into the room, noting that the TV volume was pretty high. "Hi, kiddo," he said, raising his voice to be heard.

She briefly glanced at him. "Hi."

Rebecca looked over her shoulder and gave him a fleeting smile of approval. Her fingers were on Amy's wrist. Apparently she was satisfied because she nodded. After putting the blood pressure cuff around her upper arm and pumping it up, she placed the circular part of her stethoscope in the bend of his sister's elbow. After listening for a few moments, she again nodded with satisfaction.

"So," she said, looking down at her patient. "The nurses tell me you're getting up and moving around. How's your pain? Are you able to keep it under control?"

Amy shrugged. "Yeah."

"Good." She sat on the bed. "The nurses also tell me you refuse to see your baby."

Amy's mouth tightened, but that was her only response. Her attention was riveted to the TV. Gabe reached up and hit the power button to turn it off.

"Hey, I was watching that." Amy shot him the drop-dead-bastard look.

He hadn't seen it for a while. Hadn't missed it either. "You need to listen to the doc."

"You can't tell me what to do."

"No," he said. "But I care about you. And it's in your best interest to hear her out."

He couldn't necessarily say the same for himself. Something told him he wasn't going to like what his sister had to say, because there wasn't a whole lot he could do to fix it.

"We need to talk, Amy," Rebecca said.

The teen slid down in the bed and folded her arms over her chest, in her classic passive/aggressive pose. "I don't have anything to say."

"You can't play the defiant-teenager game anymore," Rebecca said firmly. "Ignoring it won't change the fact that you have a baby now. You're responsible for a life, and I can't stand by and let you disregard that any longer."

"I'm not pregnant any more. You can't tell me what to do, either."

"I'm still your doctor and you're almost ready to leave the hospital. But I can't discharge you with a baby you won't care for. You have some decisions to make."

"No way—"

He moved to the foot of her bed. "Rebecca's right. You have to talk about this, Amy."

She glared at him. "Why can't you leave me alone?"

"Why can't you look at your baby?" Rebecca demanded.

Without answering, Amy turned her head away and stared out the window.

Gabe wanted to pull her into his lap, make her pain go away and tell her everything was going to be okay. She was still a little girl who'd somehow been thrust into a grown-up situation. Suddenly he knew Rebecca's suspicions were right.

"Your baby is—" Rebecca sighed. "He's beautiful, Amy. A perfect little boy. So tiny but strong. I could be wrong, but I think he has your chin. When he's mad he sticks that stubborn chin out and—" She laughed. "Well, suffice it to say he has a healthy set of lungs. He's so full of life."

Amy darted a quick glance at Rebecca, then turned away. "I don't care."

"Tell me about the father. Do you love him?" Rebecca put her hand on Amy's arm when her shoulders stiffened and her lips compressed. "How did you meet? Isn't it getting harder and harder, keeping everything locked up inside you?"

Amy didn't respond so Rebecca continued in her calm, soothing voice. "It's a heavy burden to carry around. Isn't it time you shared what happened to you?"

Gabe braced himself. He knew what was coming.

"Aren't you tired of keeping it to yourself? I know I am."

Slowly, Amy turned her head and stared. "What?"

"I think we share the same secret, Amy."

"I don't know what you mean."

Gabe's chest felt tight. He understood all too well even though he hadn't known that was coming. But the puzzle pieces fell into place, and the picture wasn't pretty.

Rebecca folded her hands together and rested them on her thigh. "I was sexually assaulted by a man I trusted."

"You were raped, too?" Amy whispered.

"Yes. In medical school. He was a football player and I was completely blinded by the fact that he was paying attention to me, the brainer geek. No boy had ever paid attention to me before." Her tone stayed low-key, but there was an edge of anger and betrayal clinging to the words.

Gabe felt every muscle in his body tighten. He wasn't shocked. Not really. Somewhere in the back of his mind he'd known. But hearing her say it made his blood run cold. Why hadn't she confided in him?

"It happened to me, too." Tears filled Amy's eyes and trickled down her cheeks. "I was so ashamed—"

"I know," Rebecca said. "You didn't do anything wrong."

On some level Gabe was thankful she was there because he didn't know what to say. What he wanted was five minutes alone with the sick creep who'd hurt his sister. It wouldn't change anything, but he'd feel a hell of a lot better. After that he wanted a piece of the guy who'd hurt Rebecca.

"He pushed and pushed. I told him no," Amy said, her voice breaking. "But he wouldn't listen. H-he hurt me."

"I'm so sorry this happened to you, sweetie," Rebecca said. She took Amy's hand between her own.

"It was just one time," Amy continued. "I didn't think anything could—you know. I…I tried to forget. To pretend it didn't happen. Then I missed my period. I didn't know what to do. I kept getting bigger. I felt it—him—move inside me." She turned bleak eyes on Gabe, then looked at Rebecca. "I didn't want the baby. I don't know if I can love him. The way he was conceived, how can I?"

She held Amy's hand in both of her own. "Don't make your baby a victim. He's as innocent as you are. And you have the option of giving him up for adoption. But before making that decision, you have to face the situation. If you bury your head in the sand, you leave your backside exposed."

Amy giggled through her tears. "There's a visual."

"It's true. I don't think you're giving yourself enough credit. You're capable of a whole lot of love."

"I don't know—"

"Remember, you're not alone. Your dad is there for you." Rebecca looked at Gabe and smiled reassuringly. "And your brother. I'm going to have the nurse bring in the baby so you can hold him—"

Gabe heard what she said and backed away. He couldn't face this. He wanted to be there for his sister. He *had* been there for her from the moment she showed up at his door. But watching her hold a baby in her arms was more than he could handle.

For reasons he couldn't define even if he wanted to, he felt as if he was losing his future all over again within the four walls of a hospital. All he could think about was getting out. He left the room and walked toward the elevator.

He was going to hell for sure. But the truth was that he'd already been living there for a very long time.

Two days later Rebecca peeked into Amy's hospital room and smiled. Sitting up in the chair, the teen was just handing her son off to her father who smiled lovingly as he snuggled the tiny baby to his chest for several moments before settling him in the clear plastic isolette.

"On his back, Dad," Amy cautioned.

"Since when?" He glanced over his shoulder at her. "It's not the way we used to do it."

"I've been reading. It's safer. There's a significant drop in SIDS—sudden infant death syndrome—since people aren't putting babies on their tummies."

"Okay," Carleton said, smiling at his daughter. "You're the boss."

The scene tugged at her heart. A balloon bouquet took up a corner of the room. There was a flower arrangement in a ceramic booties vase. Stuffed animals, rattles, a diaper bag and tiny clothes were scattered around. The hospital bed looked more like a display in Babies R Us with denim overalls from a name-brand company, some terry-cloth sleepers and the biggest box of newborn disposable diapers Rebecca had ever seen. Baby boy Thorne would outgrow them before he could use them all up. This picture finally looked the way it should.

She rapped her knuckles on the door frame. "Knock, knock."

Amy tore her gaze from the baby, then smiled with genuine pleasure. "Hi, Rebecca."

"Hey, you. Carleton," she said to the older man.

"If it isn't the Thorne family's favorite doctor."

Maybe these two Thornes', but not Gabe's. She hadn't seen or heard from him since coaxing Amy to confess by opening up about her own past. Rebecca wasn't prepared for the wave of pain that rolled through her when the truth hit. Gabe was gone—at least as far as she was concerned. She shouldn't have told him like that, but there wasn't time to consider his reaction when she'd realized what she had to do. And she didn't want to lose momentum or opportunity.

Her patient's welfare had been the first priority, and it

looked as if her gamble had paid off. This concerned young mother was the complete opposite of the hostile-teen-in-denial she'd first met. Maybe confession really was good for the soul. Although, in her case, not so much.

She hid her sadness behind the best smile she could produce and looked around the room. "If you'd like, I can reserve a U-Haul truck and several burly men to cart this stuff out of here for you."

Carleton laughed. "Is that your diplomatic way of saying that I'm spoiling my grandson?"

"It is if you bought all this stuff."

"Guilty as charged," he admitted, not looking the least bit repentant.

Amy sat forward in the chair and lovingly smoothed her fingers over her son's cheek. "I tried to tell him, but he won't listen to me."

"Excuse me. Did I not put that child on his back?"

"Okay, Dad. One point for you." She looked at Rebecca. "See what I'm up against?"

The warm feeling Rebecca got almost pushed away the coldness in her heart from Gabe's rejection. "All new mothers should be so lucky."

"I know. And to think I was afraid to tell him I was pregnant." She glanced at her father. "I thought he didn't want me around. I was afraid if I told him what happened, he would be even more disappointed in me than he was before."

"And you were wrong," Rebecca pointed out.

"I don't think I would have had the courage to talk about it if you hadn't told me what happened to you." She hesitated, then said, "I talked to my father about it. I hope you don't mind."

Rebecca shook her head. "If there's any lesson to be learned, it's that keeping secrets hurts the ones we love, but mostly we harm ourselves."

"I get it now," Amy said. "And when I think about what this secret could have done to my baby. If not for you—"

"Don't go there." Rebecca held up her hands. "And don't beat yourself up. What happened to you wasn't your fault and you were dealing with the consequences the best way you knew how. Believe me, I didn't handle my own consequences very well."

"Do you want to talk about it?" Carleton asked, sympathy and a new wisdom in his eyes.

"Not really." She laughed. "But then I'd be a do-as-I-say-not-as-I-do kind of person, wouldn't I?"

"If the shoe fits…" he said.

"I was engaged a couple years ago," she began. "It had been a long time since the assault and I thought I was past the point where he could hurt me anymore. The problem was I'd never told anyone."

"No one?" Amy asked.

Rebecca shook her head. She wasn't sure why she was sharing this with them, except maybe it would help Amy to deal with things better than she had. Lead by example.

"I didn't want my parents to know. Just like you," she added. "I didn't want to hurt them. And I didn't want them to know how stupid I'd been."

"It wasn't your fault," Carleton interjected. "Amy and I have been talking to the counselor together and if there's one recurring message, that's it. You just said it to her yourself."

"I know. It's something we need to keep repeating to ourselves." She smiled sadly. "The thing is, I didn't think my fiancé needed to know what happened. After all, I was over it. But then I started having nightmares and I finally told him why."

"And what did he do?" Amy asked.

"He became distant. Soon after that he broke things off. His excuse was that he wasn't prepared to handle something like that, but reading between the lines, I knew that it was just too much trouble to deal with me, what happened to me. He was ashamed of me. The message, little grasshopper," she said, trying to add levity to her words, "is that keeping secrets can cost you."

Rebecca thought she'd learned the lesson, but clearly she'd been wrong. What happened with Gabe just confirmed what she already knew—she was book smart, not street smart. But she'd believed sharing her past was on a need-to-know basis, and she'd never intended to let things with Gabe escalate to the point where he needed to know. Everything between them happened so fast. Now everything hurt so much. She'd botched it badly, and that had cost her any chance with Gabe.

Carleton put his arm around her shoulders. "The man you were going to marry is an idiot. Obviously you dodged a bullet."

The words brought tears to her eyes and she was afraid she would embarrass herself. Blinking hard she said, "I appreciate that. But I also need to take responsibility for my part. I gave what happened to me a lot of power by waiting too long to tell him."

Amy's eyebrows drew together as a troubled expression settled in her eyes. "I think I waited too long to tell Gabe."

"Why do you say that, sweetheart?" her father asked.

"Because I haven't seen him since he found out."

That was a surprise to Rebecca. "He hasn't been back to visit?"

Amy shook her head. "No."

"Probably because he knows I've been here," Carleton offered. "I know he's busy with the hospital construction project. In fact, I haven't seen him at the house, either. He's probably got an accumulation of loose ends at the office."

"You are aware that he basically works here at Mercy Medical Center?" Rebecca asked.

"Yes, but—" Carleton didn't finish that statement.

He knew as well as Rebecca did that no matter how busy Gabe was at the office, the office was close enough for him to drop in and see how his sister was doing. The thing was, it didn't make sense. The Gabe she'd come to know didn't walk out on the people he loved.

The Gabe she'd come to love had been nothing but supportive. Rebecca had shared her suspicions so Amy's tearful admission of what happened to her hadn't come as a complete shock to him. The shock would have been her own confirmation of sharing a similar experience.

She replayed that scene in her head and realized he hadn't said anything after Amy's confession. She'd asked the nurse to bring in the baby, and when she turned around he was gone. She'd figured he needed time to process the information. Then she hadn't heard from him and the realization had sunk in that she was too much trouble for him to deal with. But that was about him and her. It never crossed her mind that he hadn't been back to see his sister.

"Rebecca, speaking of that U-Haul truck," Carleton said, changing the subject, "when can I take my daughter and grandson back to Texas?"

She met his gaze. "They're both doing well. I wanted to keep her a couple more days to help her deal with being a mom, and a little more time with the counselor."

"It's helped a lot," Amy confirmed.

"It's a breakthrough," Rebecca countered. "But emotional recovery is ongoing." If anyone knew that it was her. "I would strongly urge you to find someone at home that you can talk to and continue the process."

"I've already looked into it," Carleton said.

"Good." When she looked at the two of them and the sleeping infant who was as sweet and innocent as he could be, Rebecca felt a lump in her throat. She'd grown so fond of this family. It would be hard to say goodbye. To all of them. "I'd like to keep you one more night."

"All right. Whatever you think best." Carleton smiled at his daughter. "Then we'll spend a little time with your brother while you recuperate before we go home."

Rebecca planned to spend some quality time with Gabe Thorne, too. She was sorry he'd had such a rough go of it, but that didn't automatically give him a pass to hurt people.

She was going to talk to Gabe and tell him exactly what she thought.

Chapter Fourteen

Rebecca had never been to where Gabe worked, a portable on the Mercy Medical campus that could be moved anywhere at a moment's notice. And apparently it was a metaphor for his life. He only let people in temporarily, then he was gone when someone didn't meet his expectations. She'd thought he was different and hadn't known being wrong could hurt so much.

She climbed the three steps of the portable stairway and didn't bother knocking before opening the door. Frankly, she didn't actually give a damn if she interrupted something. She walked into what looked like a reception area. There was no one at the desk, which made sense. It was after six o'clock. But she'd seen light in one of the back offices. It was probably Gabe, since his father had said he was working all the time.

She took a deep breath and moved to the open doorway,

then looked inside. When she saw him behind his desk, head bent as he read something, her heart did that funny little skip it always did. This time it was more painful than exciting. This time would be the last time, and the realization cut clear to her soul.

He glanced up and looked surprised. "Rebecca."

"You were expecting someone else?"

"No. I—" He leaned back in his chair and ran his fingers through his hair. "When the door opened I— We usually get FedEx pickup about this time. I thought you were the delivery guy."

Nope, but he was probably going to wish she was. She pulled her sweater tighter. The chilly desert wind whipped across the valley outside, but it felt colder in here. That was probably more about how she felt on the inside than anything else.

"It's just me."

"What's up?" He frowned and sat up straight, his muscles tensing. "Is it Amy? Did she have a setback?"

Rebecca noticed he didn't ask about the baby. Now that she thought about it, he'd never really discussed his nephew.

"Amy's fine. No thanks to you," she added.

"What does that mean?"

"You haven't been to see your sister for a couple of days."

"I've been busy," he said. "Work has piled up…"

"So your father said."

He held out his hand, indicating the chair in front of his desk. "Would you like to sit down?"

No. Yes. She couldn't decide if it would be easier to say what she had to say from a sitting position. Finally the trembling in her legs made the decision for her.

"Thanks," she said, and sat.

"You've seen my father?"

"He's at the hospital with his daughter and grandson all day every day." And you have his eyes, she wanted to say as she stared into the bottomless dark blue.

"He's retired," Gabe informed her, a touch of defensiveness in his tone. "He has the time."

"I'm not going to split hairs with you, Gabe. I'll get straight to the point."

"Which is?"

She folded her hands together so tightly that there was a real possibility of cutting off circulation. "Amy turned to you in her time of need."

"And I was there when she needed me."

"She still needs you."

He shook his head. "Dad's with her."

"She needs *all* her family now."

"I'm not sure what more I can do. Dad's taking her back to Texas."

That comment reeked of passing the buck. As if Amy was too much trouble now that he knew what she was dealing with. "So the fact that she'll be in a different state somehow absolves you of involvement?"

"I thought you were getting to the point," he said.

"Okay." She met his gaze without flinching. "You have issues with me. Why are you punishing your sister?"

"I'm working. That has nothing to do with my sister."

"And you can't walk the short distance to see her? You can even drop by after visiting hours because you have an official Mercy Medical badge with the handy-dandy magnetic strip that allows you in whenever you want."

If only she had a badge to swipe that could keep him out of her heart.

"It's complicated," he said, pain and guilt mixing together on his face.

"It's not complicated. You're reacting to the information that I was sexually assaulted."

Anger flashed through his eyes. "You should have told me what happened to you."

"I don't see why." That was a defensive lie. She knew now.

"I had a right to know." His expression was full of accusation.

"What difference would it have made?"

"When we were intimate— You should have—" He blew out a long breath.

"The man who raped me took my virginity, Gabe. He took something beautiful, something that I wanted to give to the man I fell in love with. He took that and left me with nothing but an ugly memory. It was mine to do with as I pleased and it pleased me to keep it to myself."

Comprehension dawned in his expression. "That's what broke up your engagement."

She nodded and was angry and mortified when her mouth trembled. Crying was not an option. When she could trust her voice, she said, "Things changed between us after I told him. He looked at me differently and wouldn't touch me. I'd worked hard to put it behind me and not feel like damaged goods and all that work was a waste because telling him put me right back to square one. In his eyes I was dirty. Then he said I was too much for him to deal with."

"You could have trusted me," Gabe said quietly.

"Yeah. Right. The way you're acting with your sister certainly inspires trust." She couldn't keep the sarcasm out of her tone and didn't have the strength to be sorry.

"It's not the same—"

She held up her hand. "The point is it was my past. It's not something you just blurt out to anyone. You were my patient's brother. I didn't think it would matter whether or not you knew. Then it mattered too much."

"Why?"

Because I love you, she wanted to say. She might have trusted him with that information once, but not now. "Forget it. The thing is, I'm here to find out why you're avoiding your sister. Do us both a favor and don't blame it on work again."

"I wasn't going to."

"Then what is it? Amy is a single teenage mother. She has a little boy who is your nephew. You have to help her—"

"No." He stood suddenly and the angles of his face seemed sharper with intensity. "I've helped her with all I can. I can't do anything for her now."

"Of course you can— The baby needs—"

"How can I do anything for the baby when I don't even want to see it?"

"What?" She couldn't believe she'd heard right.

"I don't want to see the baby," he repeated. He closed his eyes for a moment and released a shuddering breath. "And if that's not bad enough, I'm jealous of my sister."

"I don't understand."

"She didn't want her child, Rebecca. I know why now. It's not her fault. What happened to her bites, and I'd like nothing better than five minutes alone with the creep. I'm angry about what he did. And angry for myself. I can't help it. She has what I wanted more than anything in the world, and fate snatched it right out of my hands."

"What are you saying?"

"Hannah and I were going to have a baby."

She couldn't have been more shocked if he'd slapped her. Going to have a baby. Past tense. Oh, God. She whispered the question. "What happened, Gabe?"

"She was pregnant when that car plowed into her. Did you

know that a baby can only live four to five minutes inside its dead mother?" His eyes were dark with the awful memories. "Of course you do. You're a doctor. You're a smart lady."

"They had to take the baby early," she guessed.

"Right in one," he confirmed. He smiled, but it wasn't the least bit comforting. It was a dark and frightening expression. Then his gaze lost focus, as if he were somewhere else entirely. "She was a fighter." He met her gaze. "I named her Lillian, after my mother."

"Oh, Gabe—" She stood and reached out a hand, then curled her fingers into her palm and put her fist on his desk.

"Lilly lived for a week in the neonatal intensive care unit. She was a little bit bigger than the palm of my hand and had tubes everywhere. Her cry—" He stopped and shook his head. "It was so tiny. I didn't know if she was in pain, and that tore me apart because I was willing her to survive and that could have been torture. But I needed her to live. I'd just lost her mother and I wanted to keep a part of Hannah with me. I was there the whole time, watching Lilly's little chest rise and fall, listening for the beep of whatever piece of equipment was keeping her alive. Then she started to fail and there was nothing more they could do. And all I had left was silence."

"Gabe, I'm so sorry for your loss." Pathetic, inadequate words.

"I know." The intensity drained out of him and he just looked tired. "I'm sorry, too."

Rebecca was sorry for him and herself. He'd lost the will to care when his child died. She only knew about him losing Hannah and thought she understood him, but she realized she wasn't even close. She hadn't truly known hope was grasping for purchase inside her until it slipped away. The power of the pain surprised her even more, and there was no treatment that could ease the ache of being right that he could never love her. There was no comfort in the fact that it had nothing to do with her past and everything to do with his.

"Gabe, what happened to you was horrible. Worse than horrible. I can't even put it into words."

"There's a *but* coming," he said.

"No one knows better than a doctor that tragedy happens. It's part of life and if there's any positive at all, it's that people are determined to get more out of whatever time they have. Hold on to the feeling of how short our existence is, how fragile, how unfair when it's taken too soon. Some are inspired by loss."

"I'm not."

"That's too bad." She took a deep breath. "I didn't know Hannah, but she must have been extraordinarily special if you and Amy loved her so much. Something tells me she'd be really ticked off at you for hiding from life."

"Don't you dare tell me I have to go on," he said angrily. "You have no idea what it was like."

"You're right. I don't know. But you can't run away from life because of the bad stuff."

"Watch me." The words were clipped and cold.

She pulled her sweater tight around her and hated how much she wished it was his arms. "It does explain why you hate hospitals. I'm deeply sorry you didn't get your miracle, but I can't regret that Amy did."

"Now you know what a self-centered bastard I am."

"Not yet. But you're close."

His eyes narrowed. "What does that mean?"

"Hannah and your daughter, Lilly, had no choice about abandoning you. You're right about fate being responsible for that."

"Your point?"

"What you're doing to your sister is different. Your behavior is a conscious choice to abandon her and her child, your nephew. Your family. If you turn your back, it's unforgivable." She started out of his office and hesitated, then looked at him again. "I heard a saying once that stuck with me. We make a living by what we get. We make a life by what we give." She stared at him, memorizing every line, angle and shadow of his face while pain cut through her. When tears burned the back of her eyes, she willed them not to fall. It took every ounce of her self-control to keep her voice steady. "I never really understood what that meant until I met you."

After a night spent alternately remembering Rebecca telling him off and missing her, Gabe was tired. The walk down the hospital corridor toward his sister's room had never seemed so long before. He didn't necessarily agree with everything the doc had said, but one barb had hit home and stuck. He'd lost too many people he cared about. If he didn't see Amy now, the damage might be insurmountable. The rift between them was just closing, and this could tear them apart forever.

It was lunchtime and he'd called to make sure his sister hadn't been discharged. In the hallway outside her room, he stopped and steeled himself. He caught a glimpse of his father putting stuffed animals and baby clothes into bags that he set by the chair. Then he gathered balloon and flower arrangements together into a group.

Carleton's back was to the door. "I think that's everything, Amy. We just need the doctor's okay and we can go."

"Then I guess I'm just in time." Gabe took a step inside the room and looked at his sister, sitting on the bed and holding the baby.

"Gabe!"

His sister's smile lit up her face for just a moment, then disappeared. For a split second she'd looked radiant. Now hostile Amy was back, and he couldn't really blame her.

"Hi, kiddo. How are you?"

"Fine."

"Glad to hear it."

"What are you doing here?" she asked.

His father came forward and shook his hand, urging him farther into the room. "It's good of you to come by."

There was no judgment in the words, but Gabe still felt guilty. He looked at his sister. "I'm sorry I haven't been to see you sooner."

She shrugged. "No big deal."

"Yeah, it is."

"You've been busy. I understand." She clutched the bundle in her arms tighter to her chest.

They'd grown close since she'd insinuated herself into his life. He hated this distance and wanted back what they'd started to build.

"It wasn't because of work. It's me. I've been going through some stuff—" He stopped when he saw movement from the blanket in her arms. Suddenly he saw an impossibly small fist waving in the air. Then there was a series of squeaks and grunts followed by a newborn cry.

The pitifully weak wails of his daughter were carved forever into his mind and heart and he knew the difference. This child was healthy and strong, full of life.

"It's because of Lilly, isn't it?" Amy asked.

He met her gaze and nodded because he didn't think he could get words past the lump in his throat.

"I'm so sorry, Gabe," she said. "I didn't mean to bring back bad memories for you."

"I know you didn't," he said quickly. "It's not your fault. It's just—" he remembered Rebecca's words "—fate."

His father put a hand on his shoulder and squeezed. "Fate has not been kind to you, son."

He glanced from the sympathy on his father's face to the guilt on his sister's. "It hasn't been kind to any of us Thornes."

"It pretty much sucks," she admitted. "But thanks to Rebecca I've been talking to a crisis counselor here at Mercy Medical and things feel a little better." She glanced at their father. "Dad has made arrangements for me to see someone at home, too."

Gabe stood at the foot of her bed and folded his arms over his chest. "Sounds like a good idea."

"I'm also going to get my GED and apply to colleges. Dad's going to help me," she added.

It was almost as if she was telling him she didn't need him any longer. Telling him she was sorry she'd inconvenienced him. And he felt like the world's biggest jerk.

"Look, Amy, I know you came to me because you didn't believe you had anywhere else to go. I wish you'd never felt that way. I wish I could go back and have a do over. I wish I could have gotten it right the first time."

"It's okay, Gabe—"

"No, it's not." He moved beside the bed and looked down at her. He watched her take the tiny waving hand tenderly into her own and saw the love in her eyes for this baby that she hadn't wanted. He knew Rebecca was right about miracles. His family had finally gotten one within the walls of Mercy Medical Center.

"I've been a complete ass."

"Not complete," she said, one corner of her mouth curving up. "Only half."

"Okay." He laughed. "From now on, we talk things over that are bothering us. Deal?"

She nodded. "That's what I'm learning. Rebecca said she's still learning, too."

Hearing her name made his chest go tight. He remembered the disappointment in her eyes when she'd left his office last night. He'd let her down and despised himself for that.

"Learning is good." He glanced down at the infant and finally let himself really look at the baby's face. "I think he's got your chin."

Amy beamed down at her baby. "That's what Rebecca said."

Gabe remembered. Just before she'd insisted Amy hold the little guy— He didn't even know what she was going to call the child. "Have you picked out a name?"

"Matthew Gabriel." When his gaze locked with hers, doubt crept in. "I hope that's okay."

"Better than okay," he said, and heard his voice crack.

"Do you want to hold him?" she asked hesitantly.

"Yeah."

"He's small, but Rebecca says he's tough," she said, gently settling the baby in his arms when he leaned down.

Gabe snuggled the tiny, warm body close and marveled at the wonder of new life. His nephew. His family. He could almost feel his heart start up again, as if he'd been existing in suspended animation. This child wasn't the only one with new life. Gabe felt as if he'd been given another chance to live.

He wasn't sure what to do with that information since he'd made such a mess of everything with Rebecca. But come hell or high water he felt whole again, and she was the one who'd put him back together.

"So what do you think of your namesake?" his father asked, staring at the infant who was quietly looking up at Gabe.

"He's definitely a Thorne."

"If it wasn't for you, Gabe—" Amy stopped and caught her top lip between her teeth. "I can't thank you enough for what you did for me."

"It wasn't anything really," he said, fascinated by the tiny being in his arms.

"That's not true. You took me in. You took care of me. You found Rebecca." She took a deep breath. "If not for her, Matthew might not be here. Or me for that matter."

As it turned out, she had saved his sister's life, too. "The doc is pretty special."

"I owe her a lot. And I owe my big brother." Amy's eyes filled with tears.

"What is family for?" he said, looking down at her, then her child in his arms.

"Hi—" Rebecca walked in the room and stopped when she saw him holding the baby. "I didn't expect to see—" She glanced around. "I didn't mean to interrupt. I'll come back—"

"Don't go," Carleton said. "Were your ears burning?"

"Excuse me?"

"We were just talking about you."

"Oh?" Her glance touched each of them, then settled on Gabe and the baby. She smiled brightly, but it was her doctor face in place and didn't do anything to dispel the sadness in her eyes. "Should I be afraid?"

"Hardly. You are quite the heroine." His father put an arm around her. "We've decided the Thorne family owes you a great deal."

"No. It's my job." She looked at Amy. "And how are you?"

"Can Matthew and I go home?"

"After I check you over one more time, I'll sign your discharge orders." She looked at Gabe, then his father. "Gentlemen? If we could have some privacy?"

"Of course." His dad walked to the doorway. "I need to talk to Gabe, anyway."

Gabe settled little Matthew on his back in the isolette. He didn't want to leave. Partly because the family connection felt good. Partly because he hadn't seen that angry look in his father's eyes or heard that irritated tone in his voice since he'd been a rowdy teen picked up by the cops for underage drinking.

But mostly because he didn't want to leave Rebecca. And how much he didn't want to leave her scared the hell out of him more than his father ever could.

Chapter Fifteen

Gabe stood in the hall beside his father. They leaned against the wall and stared at the door to his sister's room for a few moments while hospital personnel walked back and forth. They were transporting patients in wheelchairs or moving beds or pushing sophisticated machinery that would give them information so vital to the treatment process. Miracles happened at Mercy Medical, and he'd just left one on the other side of that door.

The truth was he hadn't wanted to let go of the baby. It had felt so good to hold life in his arms and he missed the warmth. Rebecca was in there, too, and he missed her even more. He'd been missing her for a while now and was too stubborn to admit it.

He couldn't eat. He couldn't sleep. He couldn't work.

"So how are things at T&O Construction?" his father asked.

Someday he was going to have to ask the man how he did

that, but not today. He was pretty sure his father wanted to discuss something Gabe didn't really want to think about, let alone talk about. Right now the opportunity to talk about anything besides his own personal issues looked pretty damn good. So, work it was.

His father was still a limited partner in the business; it made sense he'd want to know how the project was going.

"Things are good," he answered. "The hospital expansion is on schedule and under budget, although with the rising cost of gas and materials that could change."

"But you figured a generous profit margin into the bid."

Gabe nodded. "The most significant revenue yield will be on the next campus for this hospital group. Adding on to this building was the best strategy to get our foot in the door and show them what we can do. I had a meeting this morning with the president in charge of Mercy Medical's southern Nevada market area. He's very pleased with our work ethic and the quality of construction."

His father smiled. "Have I ever told you how proud I am of you, Gabe?"

He thought about it, and for the life of him couldn't remember ever hearing those words. His mother had said it often. He vividly recalled teasing her that she was his mom and had to tell him good stuff, but she'd denied maternal feelings had anything to do with her praise.

Carleton cleared his throat. "I must assume from your silence that the answer is no."

"Yeah. It's no. I don't remember hearing that from you."

His father stared at the floor for several moments, frowning. When he looked up his blue eyes were suspiciously bright. "I apologize for that. I haven't been a very good father to you or Amy."

Gabe shook his head. "That's not true, Dad. You did the best you could—"

"Under the circumstances," he finished.

"That's not what I was going to say."

"Maybe not. But it's the truth." His father suddenly looked old. "I think I did all right while your mother was alive. We always said we were partners, a team, but the truth is that she did everything—everything that was important, I should say. I was busy expanding the business, obsessed with making it enormously successful. Lillian took care of the house and raised you to be an exceptional man."

"She was something special," Gabe agreed.

"When I lost her, it was like I died, too," his father admitted. "I'm ashamed to admit that I didn't want to go on without her. Not even for you. Especially not for a baby girl I blamed for taking my wife from me. Besides, what did I know about raising a girl?"

"Dad, you don't have to—"

Carleton touched his arm. "Yes. I do. It's way past time I talked about this. I've kept things bottled up inside for too long. It nearly cost me my daughter. I shut down, and Amy paid the price. I'm lucky. I've got a second chance and I plan to make the most of it."

"I guess the two of you have talked?"

"We have. She and the baby are coming home to live with me. That house is too big for one person anyway. It will be good to have a child there again to fill it with toys and noise and laughter."

"She's going to school?"

He held his hands up. "Completely her idea. I'm just support staff."

"How's that?"

"Babysitter." The single word put the sparkle back in his

eyes. "I'm going to take care of little Matthew Gabriel while Amy does whatever is necessary for her education. Her choice," he said firmly. "I practically ignored her when she was growing up. This is an opportunity to make it up to her, and I don't intend to screw it up by being overbearing. She's so bright, Gabe. All she needs is a helping hand. How can I not finally give her that?"

"You're not the only one who failed her, Dad. I wasn't there for her, either. It was hard losing Mom, and I guess part of me blamed Amy for that." He met his father's gaze.

"I found out hiding from the pain doesn't help."

"All you can do is acknowledge what happened and move on, Dad."

"I'm not talking about me, now. I was referring to you."

"Me?"

His father looked grim. "Son, you and I are members of a club no one wants to join."

"Dad, I don't want to talk—"

"Tough. It's way past time. *Not* talking is what we Thornes have always done. Not talking got us nowhere. It's the worst thing you can do. Trust me on that. If anyone knows how hard it was losing Hannah, it's me, Gabe." He stared hard. "And you lost your child, too. I have no idea how much hurt that caused you. And we have a conditioned response to pain. When something hurts, you do your best to avoid it."

Gabe could almost hear Rebecca saying pain is important. It's an indicator of something wrong. Then you go to the source and eliminate it. Ignoring pain is dangerous. But ignoring pain is exactly what he'd been doing.

"Gabe," his father said, "don't make the same mistakes I did."

"You're right, Dad. I have another chance to build a relationship with my sister and my nephew and I don't plan to blow it this time."

"That's good to hear, but it's not what I meant."

"Then I don't have a clue what you're talking about."

"Don't you?" Carleton looked at him. "Son, any fool can see that you're in love with Rebecca."

Gabe should have seen that coming, but he hadn't. Maybe because he didn't want to. "Dad, you've been here what? A couple of days? What do you know about it?"

"I have eyes, and they still work pretty well for an old guy. I saw the way you looked at her a few minutes ago. I know how it feels to look at a woman that way. I'm not so old that I don't remember."

"Come on, Dad." He looked up and down the corridor. No one seemed to be paying any attention to them, but this was a hell of a public place for this kind of discussion. And Rebecca would be out of that room any minute. How was he supposed to sidestep the discussion when his father had turned into Dr. Phil? "Can we talk about this later—"

"No."

"Okay, then." Gabe blew out a long breath. "I'm attracted to her."

"It's more than that and you know it. Don't be afraid, son."

"Geez, Dad."

"It's not weak to acknowledge your feelings. The things that happen to us impact our lives, but they don't need to make us less than we are. Why is it so hard for you to admit you love her?"

Gabe met his father's gaze and knew the old man wouldn't let up until he said it. "Because I don't want it to be true. I don't want to care. I don't want to lose her and ever hurt like that again."

"So you refuse to play the game?"

"There's no game to play."

"That's where you're wrong, son. The game started the

moment you saw her, and the stakes have gotten higher and higher every time since then. It's fate."

There was that word again. Fate takes and it gives back again. Keeping balance in the universe.

"Even if you're right, and I'm not admitting you are, that doesn't mean she feels the same way."

"I saw the way she looked at you, too."

They'd already established that he had pretty good eyesight for an old guy. "So, what if you're right?"

"I think you know how fond I was of Hannah. She was a firecracker as a little girl and she grew into a fine woman. The world is worse off for not having her in it. And she loved you with all her heart. That is how I know she would be the first to encourage you to embrace life and find happiness with a fine woman like Rebecca."

Something cracked inside Gabe. It felt like walls tumbling down inside him, and he could finally see clearly what had been just beyond them. Or maybe he'd just been waiting for permission to let go. He'd been so focused on protecting himself that he never realized he'd started to care more about someone else than himself.

In the painful struggle of self-protection, he'd walked away from Rebecca just like the jerk who'd hurt her. But that guy had been so wrong. Rebecca wasn't too much trouble. Gabe had no trouble at all falling in love with her.

The door to his sister's room opened and he saw the woman he loved. Before she put on her doctor face, he thought he saw sadness in her eyes. Then she smiled.

"She's doing great, Carleton. I'm going to sign the paperwork now so you can take her and the baby home."

"Thank you for everything, Rebecca."

"You're very welcome."

Gabe stepped closer. "Rebecca, if you have a minute—"

She took a step back. "Actually, I don't. I have patients to see. If you'll excuse me." She glanced between them. "Don't hesitate to call my office if you have any questions. I told Amy the same thing. I have to run. Bye."

Then she turned and hurried down the hall, turning right at the end toward the elevators.

Gabe stared at the empty space where she'd been just moments before. "About Rebecca, I've got a serious problem. She thinks I'm the world's biggest jerk."

His father clapped a hand on his shoulder. "Every problem has a solution, son. But if you let her go without trying, you're lower than a jerk. You're a spineless coward who doesn't deserve her."

In spite of everything Gabe grinned. "Don't sugarcoat it, Dad. Tell me how you really feel."

"I'm on your side."

"Thanks for clarifying. It was hard to tell."

And it would be hard to convince Rebecca that he deserved another chance. She was smart. But so was he. And he would come up with something because failure wasn't an option. He'd lost too much in his life to give up without a fight.

And he'd been wrong about something else. Mercy Medical was the perfect place for this discussion with his father. It was a place of healing mind, body and spirit.

Rebecca walked along the sidewalk under the portico toward Mercy Medical's front door. It whooshed open, allowing her entrance to the two-story rotunda with the information desk on the right. She looked around. The floor was still marble tile. The yellow rose painting was still on the wall and artfully lighted. Over the arch, the same words were inscribed. Hospital personnel walked back and forth, working together for the patients.

Nothing looked different, but something was and she couldn't put her finger on what. Then she realized. The hospital no longer felt safe to her, because she'd changed after losing Gabe in this place.

Considering what she'd been through, she was finding it more difficult to believe that miracles happened within these four walls. At least, there would be no miracle for her. And if that wasn't enough of a personal pity party, today she was giving her monthly workshop on the risks and prevention of teenage pregnancy. There was no reason to believe the turnout would be better than any of the others she'd conducted.

She walked over to the information desk. "Hi, Sister Mary. How are you?"

"Dr. Hamilton." The older woman looked up and smiled, then settled her glasses more securely on her nose. "I'm very well, thanks. And you?"

"Not bad." Not good, but she didn't intend to talk to a nun about her loser love life. "I'm here for my workshop. I guess it's in the McDonald conference room?"

"Actually, no." The sister looked down at a sheet in front of her. "We had to move you."

To a broom closet? Rebecca wanted to ask. She'd never needed more room than that. In fact the last person to show up had been a couple months ago. She felt a sharp stab of pain in her heart when she remembered it was Gabe. And he'd come because he wanted information about his sister. Now he was out of her life.

"So where did you put me?" she asked before going straight to the bad place.

"You're in the St. Rose conference room."

Rebecca stared at her. They'd moved her to the biggest meeting area? "Are you sure?"

"Yes. There were too many people for the McDonald room.

On the bright side, there won't be any confusion between you and fast food."

"Are you positive there's not a mix-up? Is there a health fair today? Maybe all the people are here for free ice cream and a cholesterol screening?"

Sister Mary tsked. "Now, dear. You're too young to be so cynical."

"Sorry, sister." But if she only knew, Rebecca thought. "Maybe the board of directors did a promotion or some advertising in the *Women's Magazine*."

"Did you give the information to the public relations staff?"

"No."

"Then that's not it." Sister Mary shrugged. "Don't look a gift horse in the mouth, dear."

"Okay. Thanks, sister."

Rebecca took the elevator upstairs. When she passed the Labor and Delivery waiting room, she glanced over, then did a double take. In a discreetly lighted corner alcove sat the graceful sculpture of a woman that Gabe had purchased at the silent auction the night of the Southern Nevada Rape Crisis Center fundraiser. She moved closer and read the plaque beneath the lovely piece of art. "In memory of Lillian Thorne and Hannah O'Neill. Donated by Gabriel Thorne."

Her breath caught; her hands shook. He was an incredibly nice man who'd done an incredibly emotional thing and given her one more reason not to feel safe. Every day when she walked through the doors to see her patients, she would be reminded that he couldn't love her because his heart was broken.

She continued on and walked into the conference room, which was filled with people milling around and chatting in groups. There were men and women, teenage boys and girls. As she scanned everyone, her gaze settled on the one man she'd never expected to see again, let alone here.

Gabe.

When he saw her, his eyes darkened as the corners of his mouth turned up in a grin that made her stomach drop as if she were an unwilling passenger on a freefalling elevator. She lifted her hand and gave him a small wave before taking her place at the lectern. Seeing him again made her miss him more. And it almost made her forget to wonder why he was there. He wasn't a teen and he couldn't get pregnant. But, of course, part of her workshop was dedicated to making the boys aware of and accountable for their actions.

"Thank you all for coming." No one paid any attention.

Gabe put his fingers to the sides of his mouth and blew out a shrill whistle. Everyone stopped talking and looked at her.

"Thanks for coming," she repeated. "I'm really happy to see such a large turnout. If you'd all find seats, we'll begin."

She was shaking really hard. It had nothing to do with talking in front of all these people and everything to do with the man who would own her heart forever. Forcing herself to concentrate, she tried to remember her notes.

"Abstinence and responsibility," she began.

If she didn't look at Gabe, she was almost able to forget he was there. She talked about refraining from sex being the most reliable method of avoiding pregnancy. Next she touched on using condoms as a responsible method of preventing not only conception, but also STDs, sexually transmitted diseases. Then she explained the risks of pregnancy for teenagers. It wasn't in her notes, but there were boys and men who would and should be talking to their sons about what it means when a girl says no. There's never an excuse for misinterpreting or misunderstanding the word. After taking questions, she thanked everyone for coming before they filed out of the room.

When one of the last men was on his way out the door she asked him how he'd heard about the workshop.

There was what could only be called a pregnant pause before he looked guilty, then glanced at Gabe.

"I work for T&O construction," he said. "The boss asked me to come. As a favor to him."

"I see." She met his gaze. "What about the others?"

He shrugged. "I don't know all of them."

"But some?"

"Some," he admitted. He glanced at Gabe and slid him a "sorry, buddy" look before hurriedly leaving.

She wasn't sure whether to be angry or grateful for his interference. Wrong thing, right reason? Right thing, wrong reason?

Gabe walked up to her. "Hi."

"So you're responsible for all these people showing up?" she asked.

He slid his fingertips into the pockets of his jeans. "I may have had a small influence."

"Small?" She glanced around the large room that had been standing-room-only a few minutes before. "What did you do? Give them a bonus?"

"I might have made it worth their while," he admitted.

"You bribed them?"

"*Bribe* is such a negative word."

Definitely wrong thing. But for what reason? "I didn't need a pity audience."

"Amy and the baby are settling in with my Dad," he said, ignoring her self-righteous indignation.

"I'm glad. Thank you for letting me know." She picked up her purse and started to leave.

"Rebecca, don't go."

"There's no reason to stay," she argued.

"You're wrong."

"I don't think so."

"The thing is," he said, "you can run, but you can't hide. Not really."

She looked up at him. "What? Now you're an authority on interpersonal relationships?"

"Not an authority. But I know the retreat-and-hide symptoms like the back of my hand. They've been my two best friends since Hannah and Lilly died." He ran his fingers through his hair and looked away for a moment. "If it hadn't been for you, I'd still be looking the other way and wandering aimlessly through the shadows."

Her heart started beating so fast she swore it was going to burst out of her chest. "Okay. I'll give you that one. I understand hiding. I've been there, too. Other than that, I don't think we have anything more to say to each other."

"Maybe *we* don't, but I do."

She was afraid to hear this. His message had come through loud and clear, and she'd gotten it. She hurt like hell but she understood. She'd also seen him since and managed to preserve her dignity. But if she had to see him tell her to her face that he couldn't love her, she would start to cry. She was a doctor and she definitely cared more than enough to cry. She'd also never forgive him if he made her cry in front of him.

"I'm sorry, Gabe. I have to run—" Bad choice of words. She didn't miss the irony and sighed in resignation. "Okay. What do you want to say?"

He met her gaze, and his own turned dark with intensity. "I'll make this quick. It's pretty simple really. I've loved two women in my life."

Great. Because it didn't hurt enough that he couldn't love her, he had to tell her about the ones he'd never have. "Gabe, I'm really not sure—"

He touched a finger to her mouth. "I've loved two women.

I lost the first to fate. I probably lost the second by choosing not to participate."

She'd accused him of not participating. Was he saying what she thought he was? Was he saying that he loved her? She opened her mouth, but words wouldn't come out because her throat was too dry. She cleared it and said, "Thanks for the share."

"I don't blame you for being angry," he said. "But if you'll give me another chance, I promise I'll be there for you. Always."

Rebecca knew that declaration from anyone else would be subject to speculation. But not from Gabe. He had proven that he was capable of deep and abiding love for those he'd lost and the family he was committed to.

"I need you, Rebecca. I don't want to lose you." He closed his eyes for a moment, then looked at her. "You breathed life into my heart again."

There it was. Right out in the open. And he was waiting for a response. And she was afraid. She had so many scars inside it was like a road map to disaster.

When she didn't respond, he said, "I don't blame you for being scared. But I'm not that creep who hurt you. He's obviously a shallow, self-indulgent jerk who didn't really love you. If you believe nothing else, believe this. I love you. I don't deserve you, but I love you so much."

"Gabe, you're not—"

He put his hands on her arms. "You need to know that even though I don't deserve you I'm selfish enough to overlook that and pursue you until you can't resist me."

"Okay. I give."

He blinked. "What?"

"I give up. I can't resist you." She smiled as happiness filled her until it overflowed and tears of joy trickled down her cheeks. "Don't let it go to your head. And it's not a snap decision. I couldn't resist you from the first moment I saw you."

The grin was all gorgeous and macho. The look was all Gabe. "Really?"

"Really. And believe me I tried to outsmart my heart and use my superior IQ to reason my way out of being attracted to you."

He hadn't asked to fall in love any more than she had, but he was reaching out, taking a risk. How could she not do the same and meet him halfway?

"The problem is," she continued, "I fell in love with you."

"Then the smart thing to do would be to marry me." He pulled her into his arms and released a shuddering breath, so full of emotion it took any swagger out of that statement.

"Brilliant suggestion," she agreed. "Who's the brainer geek now?"

"Are you flirting with me, Doctor?"

"Is it working?"

When he kissed her she knew it was working far better than she'd ever dared hope. And she didn't feel the slightest guilt about having randy thoughts in the same room where she'd just advocated abstinence and responsibility. She and Gabe were finally taking responsibility for their feelings and had just promised to spend the rest of their lives together definitely *not* abstaining.

* * * * *

Look for LAST WOLF WATCHING
by Rhyannon Byrd—the exciting conclusion
in the BLOODRUNNERS *miniseries*
from Silhouette Nocturne.

Follow Michaela and Brody on their fierce journey to find
the truth and face the demons from the past, as they reach
the heart of the battle between the Runners and the rogues.

Here is a sneak preview of book three,
LAST WOLF WATCHING.

Michaela squinted, struggling to see through the impenetrable darkness. Everyone looked toward the Elders, but she knew Brody Carter still watched her. Michaela could feel the power of his gaze. Its heat. Its strength. And something that felt strangely like anger, though he had no reason to have any emotion toward her. Strangers from different worlds, brought together beneath the heavy silver moon on a night made for hell itself. That was their only connection.

The second she finished that thought, she knew it was a lie. But she couldn't deal with it now. Not tonight. Not when her whole world balanced on the edge of destruction.

Willing her backbone to keep her upright, Michaela Doucet focused on the towering blaze of a roaring bonfire that rose from the far side of the clearing, its orange flames burning with maniacal zeal against the inky black curtain of the night. Many of the Lycans had already shifted into their preternatural shapes, their fur-covered bodies standing like monstrous shadows at the edges of the forest as they waited with restless expectancy for her brother.

Her nineteen-year-old brother, Max, had been attacked by a rogue werewolf—a Lycan who preyed upon humans for food. Max had been bitten in the attack, which meant he was no longer human, but a breed of creature that existed between the two worlds of man and beast, much like the Bloodrunners themselves.

The Elders parted, and two hulking shapes emerged from the trees. In their wolf forms, the Lycans stood over seven feet tall, their legs bent at an odd angle as they stalked forward. They each held a thick chain that had been wound around their inside wrists, the twin lengths leading back into the shadows. The Lycans had taken no more than a few steps when they jerked on the chains, and her brother appeared.

Bound like an animal.

Biting at her trembling lower lip, she glanced left, then right, surprised to see that others had joined her. Now the Bloodrunners and their family and friends stood as a united force against the Silvercrest pack, which had yet to accept the fact that something sinister was eating away at its foundation—something that would rip down the protective walls that separated their world from the humans'. It occurred to Michaela that loyalties were being announced tonight—a separation made between those who would stand with the Runners in their fight against the rogues and those who blindly supported the pack's refusal to face reality. But all she could focus on was her brother. Max looked so hurt…so terrified.

"Leave him alone," she screamed, her soft-soled, black satin slip-ons struggling for purchase in the damp earth as she rushed toward Max, only to find herself lifted off the ground when a hard, heavily muscled arm clamped around her waist from behind, pulling her clear off her feet. "Damn it, let me down!" she snarled, unable to take her eyes off her brother as the golden-eyed Lycan kicked him.

Mindless with heartache and rage, Michaela clawed at the arm holding her, kicking her heels against whatever part of her captor's legs she could reach. "Stop it," a deep, husky voice grunted in her ear. "You're not helping him by losing it. I give you my word he'll survive the ceremony, but you have to keep it together."

"Nooooo!" she screamed, too hysterical to listen to reason. "You're monsters! All of you! Look what you've done to him! How dare you! *How dare you!*"

The arm tightened with a powerful flex of muscle, cinching her waist. Her breath sucked in on a sharp, wailing gasp.

"Shut up before you get both yourself and your brother killed. I will *not* let that happen. Do you understand me?" her captor growled, shaking her so hard that her teeth clicked together. "Do you understand me, Doucet?"

"Damn it," she cried, stricken as she watched one of the guards grab Max by his hair. Around them Lycans huffed and growled as they watched the spectacle, while others outright howled for the show to begin.

"That's enough!" the voice seethed in her ear. "They'll tear you apart before you even reach him, and I'll be damned if I'm going to stand here and watch you die."

Suddenly, through the haze of fear and agony and outrage in her mind, she finally recognized who'd caught her. *Brody*.

He held her in his arms, her body locked against his powerful form, her back to the burning heat of his chest. A low, keening sound of anguish tore through her, and her head dropped forward as hoarse sobs of pain ripped from her throat. "Let me go. I have to help him. *Please*," she begged brokenly, knowing only that she needed to get to Max. "Let me go, Brody."

He muttered something against her hair, his breath warm against her scalp, and Michaela could have sworn it was a single word…. But she must have heard wrong. She was too upset. Too furious. Too terrified. She must be out of her mind. Because it sounded as if he'd quietly snarled the word *never*.

HARLEQUIN® Romance®

Western Weddings

Jason Welborn was convinced that his business
partner's daughter, Jenny, had come to claim her share
in the business. But Jenny seemed determined to win
him over, and the more he tried to push her away, the
more feisty Jenny's response. Slowly but surely she
was starting to get under Jason's skin....

Look for

Coming Home to the Cattleman

by

JUDY CHRISTENBERRY

Available May wherever you buy books.

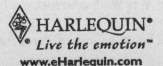

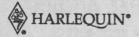

REQUEST YOUR FREE BOOKS!

2 FREE NOVELS PLUS 2 FREE GIFTS!

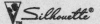

SPECIAL EDITION®

Life, Love and Family!

Silhouette

SPECIAL EDITION™

♥✚ THE WILDER FAMILY
Healing Hearts in Walnut River

Social worker Isobel Suarez was proud to work at Walnut River General Hospital, so when Neil Kane showed up from the attorney general's office to investigate insurance fraud, she was up in arms. Until she melted in his arms, and things got very tricky...

Look for

HER MR. RIGHT?
by
KAREN ROSE SMITH

Available May wherever books are sold.

V Silhouette®

COMING NEXT MONTH